This book is dedicated to you. Yes, you!
The first book was dedicated to you too, so now
you have TWO books dedicated to you.
You truly are a fancy pants.

Friday, 23rd December – 6.25pm (AKA CHRISTMAS EVE EVE)

MERRY CHRISTMAS EVE EVE! AKA the day before Christmas Eve, so I call it Christmas Eve Eve. Technically my birthday, which is the 12th December, is Christmas Eve Eve Eve Eve Eve Eve Eve Eve Eve Eve Eve Eve Eve (yep, that's thirteen Eves!) but that would take TOO long to say, especially because I speak slowly anyway!

I speak slowly because I have a disability called cerebral palsy, which just means that my muscles don't work as quickly as other people's muscles. It also means that I wobble when I walk, and I sometimes fall over . . . my knees are *always* covered in bruises!

I love Christmas. I love presents, I love putting on my pyjamas, getting cosy by the fire and watching Christmas movies, I love eating roast potatoes, I love eating my entire bodyweight in chocolate and Brussels sprouts.

My best friend Oscar says I'm weird for liking sprouts because they smell like farts! But my Dad, who is the best home cook in the entire world, makes great ones. They're crispy, and nutty, and last Christmas I ate twenty! To be fair to Osc, I did fart a lot that evening.

'What are you thinking about, Edie?' Flora asks me. She's in the seat to my right, her hand resting under her chin as she smiles. 'You look like you're on Planet Edie.'

I dunk a chip in the gravy in front of me. 'I'm thinking about Brussels sprouts!'

Everybody at the dining table laughs, because it's 'so Edie' to be thinking about food, while we're at dinner, eating food. But it's true, I blooming love food. All kinds of food. Apart from anchovies. They're Gross with a capital G!

I jump in my rocket and leave Planet Edie, and join everybody at the table on Planet Earth. Oscar (my best friend in the whole wide world) and Flora (my second amazing friend, who I met earlier this year when I started secondary school) have come to my house for tea. We're having fish and chips from the chip shop. It's a tradition on Christmas Eve Eve. Yum, yum, yum, get in my tum!

Along with my fish and chips I have been drinking so much lemonade, and suddenly I really need to go to the loo. This is part of my disability too; I often go from not needing a wee at all to suddenly being SUPER DUPER DESPERATE. I wiggle a bit in my chair.

3

'Do you need a wee?' Oscar asks. He's seen my wee dance a million times before. 'Do you need help to get to the toilet?'

'She's all right,' Flora answers, before I can. 'If she needs help, she'll ask for it.'

Oscar nods, and nobody knows this but me, but I think Oscar is a little bit annoyed at Flora. They don't know each other super well, and sometimes I think they are *very different* from each other. Oscar, like me, talks to everybody and anybody, and Flora is a little quieter and it takes her a while to open up to people. And Oscar wants to help me all of the time, but Flora likes me to do things for myself. I guess, in a way, they're both right.

'Thanks, Osc, but I think I can make it to the loo on my own.'

I smile at both of them and I jiggle to the toilet as quick as I can.

☆☆☆

After dinner, me and Mum drop Oscar and Flora back at their houses. I sit next to Flora in the car and Oscar sits up front next to my mum, chatting away. I usually sit next to my mum but I really want to sit next to Flora today. I rest my head on her shoulder.

The radio is on and it's playing Christmas hits. We all sing along at the top of our lungs. Outside it's grey and miserable, but Mum has the heat blasted up high and we have blankets. We're tucking into a box of Quality Street chocolates, and I am eating all of the strawberry ones. They're my favourite. Flora is making a collage with the shiny rainbow wrappers on our laps. Flora is brilliant and super artsy – last term she decorated the stage for the school play A Christmas Carol. I played Scrooge, the main character, who is normally a man, but last minute I decided to play Scrooge as a grumpy WOMAN, and everybody said it was brilliant. I loved being on stage, and I loved acting. I've always wanted to be a writer when I grow up but who knows . . . now I think I might want to be an actor!

I smile to myself. I feel so happy and so lucky to be in the car with some of my favourite people. I think if I could choose to stay in this moment or fast forward to Christmas Eve, I might choose this! It might be even better than the twenty-one Brussels sprouts I'm aiming to eat!

I'm quite sad that the night is over. I love being with Flora and Oscar. I really want them to get on so we can all hang out, and maybe even live together one day. How cool would that be?

As soon as I have that thought, we turn the corner and we can see Oscar's drive. Mum pulls up and Oscar jumps out of the car.

'Merry Christmas, Edie! I'll call you tomorrow!' Oscar yells, walking up the driveway. He turns back and waves, wrapping his big scarf around his neck, before the front door opens.

We drive off. Flora holds my hand and it feels like there's a little elf bouncing up and down in my tummy. For some reason I feel a little bit nervous.

When we get to Flora's house, she kisses me on my cheek and says she'll text me soon, then closes the car door. I smile and watch her walk away. It's weird. I don't know how, but I already miss her.

My mum looks at me in the rear-view mirror.

'I really like Flora, love!' she says.

'Me too.'

'Remember, you can always talk to me about anything, mushroom.'

'I know, Mum. Thanks.' I unwrap one final chocolate. I don't know why, maybe it's the sugar, but I feel very, very, very happy.

Saturday 1.35pm – CHRISTMAS EVE!

My mum is busy peeling potatoes for the dinner tomorrow. It's Christmas Eve and Grandad Eric has just walked into the kitchen with four supermarket bags full of clothes and presents plus a couple of wheelie suitcases. He's wearing one of his famous Christmas jumpers. It has a huge Rudolph on the front, and when you squeeze the red nose it plays 'Rudolph the Red-Nosed Reindeer'.

Last year, my little brother Louie found Grandad's jumper so funny. He kept squeezing the nose and running away. By the end of the day we'd heard that tune over fifty times. When I went to bed, the song was even in my dream!

Grandad Eric is only staying at our house until the day after Boxing Day, but looking at the stuff he's brought, it looks like he's planning on staying for three months.

'Is the kettle on, Angela love? I'm gasping for a brew.'

My mum gives him an angry look before picking up another potato from the counter.

8

Grandad Eric looks at me and grins. He knows he's being cheeky. 'On second thoughts, I'll make it myself!'

He pours three cups of tea – one for Mum, one for him, and one for me with a little bit of sugar.

We all sit at the kitchen table, and Grandad Eric pulls out a tin of biscuits from one of his bags. He opens the lid and chooses a custard cream, Mum chooses a Bourbon and I choose a shortbread. Delicious with a capital D!

'So when is the next spectacular performance from the Amazing Edie Eckhart?' Grandad Eric asks me.

I laugh and shrug. 'I don't know, Grandad. Hopefully soon. I really enjoyed playing Scrooge.'

'Oh love, you were marvellous too,' Mum says. She grins. 'You'd better invite me to all the ceremonies when you become a famous actor!'

I smile, but suddenly I feel a bit worried. What if I was only good at playing one character? I don't know if I'm good enough to play lots of different characters, like proper actors do.

'Me too!' Grandad Eric agrees. 'I quite fancy that Judi Dench. I'd like to meet her and give her a smooch!'

'Dad!' Mum groans, slapping Grandad Eric playfully on the arm. 'That is too much information!'

Grandad Eric laughs and winks at me. 'You made me proud up there, kid. You were brilliant.'

I smile and I give him a huge hug. I hope I can make him proud again.

Sunday 1pm – CHRISTMAS DAY

'MUMMY, I LOVE IT! I LOVE IT, I LOVE IT, I LOVE IT!' Louie screams at the top of his voice.

Because he is the youngest, Louie opens his present first. Mum and Dad have got him a bright red bike, with stabilisers, and a matching red helmet.

'Woah, fella, maybe don't ride it in the house!' Dad leaps over to Louie, who is already trying to climb on to the bike. 'Maybe we should go outside with it, yeah?'

Louie nods enthusiastically and Dad pushes the new bike out of the living room. Louie squeals with excitement and hugs me on his way out. 'Didi, this might be the best Christmas EVER!'

Louie calls me 'Didi' because when he was little he found it difficult to say 'Edie'. I like it though. It's a nice nickname.

'And this is for you, mushroom.' Mum hands me a square present, wrapped in red shiny paper and tied with a gold ribbon.

I carefully open it. I hate ripping wrapping paper, so I try to be as neat as possible.

It's a notebook! But, like, the fanciest notebook I've ever seen. It's bright purple, and in the bottom right-hand corner it has my name, *Edie Eckhart*, embossed in gold. It's beautiful.

'Oh Mum, I love it!'

'Maybe you could write stories or poems in it. You haven't written anything like that in ages!'

Mum's right. In primary school I used to write loads

of poems and stories and stuff, but since starting
secondary school I haven't done it as much. My
first term of Year 7 was busy though, and I was
distracted by the play, and making friends,
and meeting Flora . . .

'I will.' I nod, flicking through the bright white pages.
'Thanks, Mum. I love you.'

'Love you too, mushroom. Merry Christmas!' Mum
hugs me.

'WATCH THE WALL!' we hear Dad yell from outside.
Me and Mum run to the front door to see what's
happening.

Louie is on the floor and has just fallen off his bike.
But instead of crying or being upset, he is laughing. 'I
love my bike *so much!*' Louie yells to us, picking the bike
up and climbing right back on it.

Me and Mum laugh. 'Well I don't know where he gets
it from,' my mum says, 'but that brother of yours is an
absolute daredevil!'

I'm FaceTiming Oscar while lying on my bed, propped up with my pillows. Every time I move, it hurts.

'I'm dying, Oscar. Please will you do a speech for me at my funeral?'

Oscar laughs and props his phone up on his desk and spins round on his swivel chair. 'You're not dying, mate, you've just eaten too much. How many chocolates have you had from the Eckhart snowman tin?'

I count them up in my head. All the strawberry ones, all the caramel ones and a few of the toffee ones that get stuck in your teeth.

'Maybe fifteen? No, wait, I forgot to count the nut ones. I think I had eighteen!'

'And how many sprouts?!'

'I made it to twenty again. I wanted to beat my record, but Grandad Eric kept passing me his honey-roasted carrots because he doesn't like them but didn't want Mum to know! I have a belly full to the brim with veggies!'

'Ha, ha, classic Eric. The man, the legend! At least you

14

had a roast dinner. My mum thought it would be fun to have Christmas dinner pie! She literally put everything from the roast into a pie. Including the pigs in blankets! I half expected to find a bit of Christmas pudding under the pastry.'

I burst out laughing. Oscar is hilarious.

'What's your favourite present?' I ask him.

Without saying anything, Oscar jumps up from his chair and picks something up from his bed. It's a big box and I can't really see what it is.

'What's that then, Osc?' I ask.

'It's a milk frother.' Oscar answers excitedly.

'Nope. Still don't know what that is. Why would you want to froth milk?'

'It's a fancy hot chocolate maker! It makes such smooth, chocolatey hot chocolate – look!'

He holds a big mug of hot chocolate up to the camera and takes a gigantic, noisy slurp. When he takes the mug away from his mouth, he has a big brown frothy hot chocolate mark on his top lip. It looks like a moustache.

'Hello! I'm a man with a moustache!' Oscar bellows in

a deep voice. I fall apart laughing.

Oscar wipes away the moustache with the sleeve of his jumper. 'What did you get for Christmas?'

I hold up my notebook proudly.

'Of course! Another writing book for Edie the writer!' Oscar says. 'Do you promise to still be my best friend even when you're a super-famous author?'

'Osc, don't be silly! We'll always be friends!'

'Promise?'

'I promise!'

Just then, I see Charlie, Oscar's older (and often moody) sister, walk into his room.

'Charlie! Why do you never knock?'

Charlie ignores him.

'Happy Christmas, Edie,' she mumbles. 'Come downstairs, Oscar. Mum and Dad want to play Monopoly.'

Charlie is super bossy. I'm glad she's not my sister. I never boss Louie around like that.

Oscar turns to me on FaceTime. I can tell he has no choice but to go with Charlie. She has her arms crossed and clearly isn't budging from the doorway.

'If I don't chat to you tonight, I'll see you tomorrow at yours. Merry Christmas!'

'Yes, see you tomorrow! Merry Christmas back at you!'

Once I've ended the call, I pick up my new notebook.

I suppose if I want to be the 'super-famous author' Oscar thinks I'll be when I grow up, I do *actually* need to start writing things.

I decide I'll start writing tomorrow. It's Christmas Day after all. I can hear Grandad Eric's jumper from upstairs. Time for one last chocolate . . .

Monday 1.21pm

'Grandad Eric?' Louie turns to him with wide eyes. 'Why is Boxing Day called Boxing Day?'

'Because it is the day when grandparents get into a boxing ring and punch other grandparents!' Grandad Eric gets up out of his chair at the kitchen table and punches the air. Louie's eyes widen even further.

'Not really, Lou,' I reassure him, pinching his cheek. 'Grandad Eric is being a silly billy!'

Louie giggles and eats a sausage roll from his plate. 'Silly billy!'

The doorbell goes and Dad gets up.

Sausage rolls. Scotch Eggs. Crisps. Quiche. Pineapple on sticks. We always have a 'beige buffet' on Boxing Day. Otherwise known as the dinner of heroes. I couldn't be happier.

'We have an Oscar-shaped visitor,' Dad announces as he walks back into the kitchen, with Oscar trailing after him in a hat, scarf, gloves and what looks like three jumpers. I can't even see his eyes under the hat.

Maybe I *could* be happier, especially now my best friend is here! 'Hi, Osc,' I say, standing up and offering him a pineapple stick. He takes it and shivers.

'Is it chilly out, Oscar?' Grandad Eric asks.

His cheeks are red from the cold. Oscar nods, and eats.

'Why don't you go into the living room and get cosy. You could choose a film, and I'll bring you some more food?' my mum asks.

What a brilliant plan. I love my mum for suggesting it!

'Thanks, Mrs E!' Oscar grins. 'Did you have a nice Christmas Day?'

'I did, Oscar love. I was very spoilt! Edie did all of the washing up.'

'Really?' Oscar raises an eyebrow. 'So most of the water ended up on the floor then?'

My mum laughs. 'Not *all* of the water, but the kitchen floor did get a bit of a wash too!'

'If you don't want me to help, I won't next year,' I say, holding up my hands.

My mum plants a kiss on my cheek. 'Darling, I love you, and your wobbly hands. Now go in the living room and choose what film to watch.'

We decide to watch *Fantastic Four* – one of our joint faves. We sit on the sofa under a blanket with the beige buffet now perfectly located on the coffee table in front of us.

'I talked to Georgia yesterday, and she said she missed being my girlfriend.'

Georgia is lovely and she went out with Oscar for most of the last term. They broke up near Christmas because Oscar thought that he should go out with me, which is sooooooo silly because OBVIOUSLY we're just meant to be friends. The idea of kissing Oscar makes me feel gross.

'So now I guess we're going out again!' Oscar says. His cheeks go red.

I'm glad that he's going out with Georgia. At first, I'd been a bit jealous of her – it had always been me and Osc against the world, since forever, and suddenly he had a new person to hang out with. But starting secondary school has made me realise that it is OK to have lots of different friends. No matter how many friends we have, Oscar and I will always be best friends.

Flora pops into my head now. I like her, I think in the same way that Oscar likes Georgia. Does this mean that Flora should be my *girlfriend*? I'm not sure how I feel about that.

'I'm really happy for you, Oscar! I love Georgia.'

I haven't told Oscar about Flora kissing me at the play. Now would be the perfect time. I hope he's happy for me.

'Do you watch films when you hang out with Flora?' Oscar asks me, grabbing a sausage roll (our favourite food in the entire world).

'Sometimes. But mostly we just chat. Why?'

'I don't know.' Oscar replies. 'I just think you're different when you're with Flora.'

What a weird thing to say. Does different mean bad? It doesn't sound great, and it isn't something you would say about a friend you like. Wait a minute . . . does Oscar *hate* Flora?

I don't know if I want to ask what Oscar means by that, so instead of saying anything, I eat a Scotch egg and turn the volume up on the TV. I decide not to tell him about the kiss. It feels odd to tell him now, and I worry that it would make him angry or sad or something.

We watch the rest of the film without talking.

Tuesday 10.02am

On the day after Boxing Day every year we go to the beach. It's now a tradition. We wrap up warm and we wear thick gloves and eat ice cream on the seafront. It's funny, eating something so cold when it's freezing, but we wear a million layers and we make sure to warm up when we get home with hot chocolate and the remaining mince pies left over from Christmas Day.

This morning, my mum told me that I could invite my friends. I got excited by the idea of spending the day with Oscar and Flora. But then I remembered what Oscar had said yesterday. If Oscar thinks I'm different around Flora, then he probably won't want us to go to the beach together. It makes me sad to think that Oscar might dislike Flora.

Oscar came with us last year, so maybe Flora should come today.

> **Hey Flora! We're going to the beach today.**
> **Do you want to come? Xx**

I don't press send. I think about it and I decide to delete it.

Instead, I text Oscar. He'd feel left out if we went without him and I took a new friend.

> **Oscar! Do you want to come to the beach? Xx**

I delete it too.

'Knock, knock,' my dad says, coming into my room.

'Saying "knock, knock" isn't the same as actually knocking on the door, Dad!' I say, laughing. He always does this.

He laughs too. 'Sorry, missus,' he says, launching himself on my bed. 'So tell me, which of your fab friends have we got joining us? Mr Oscar and Miss Flora?'

'I've decided not to invite either of them. I think we should have an Eckhart Day.'

I sit up and kiss my dad's cheek. It's rough and stubbly.

He smiles. 'You, Edie Eckhart, are a genius. What a brilliant plan! The original gang off to the beach.'

'But, Dad, before we leave, please can you have a shave!'

Dad pretends to be angry and tickles me until we're both laughing so much it hurts. It's going to be an EPIC Eckhart Day.

6.06pm

OK, here goes. Edie Eckhart, the writer, is back in action. Starting with a poem. I think about today, open my rainbow notebook and write:

Chips by the Sea
Crispy chips,
Golden and hot,
Tangy with vinegar,
I eat the lot!

I open the paper,

'Edie! Tea's ready!' my mum shouts.
I'll finish the poem later.

Wednesday 4.52pm

It's that time between Christmas and New Year when I have no clue what day it is. I've eaten too many mince pies to really know what days of the week are any more. I've never been more thankful for my diary to make me keep track!

My dad and Louie went on a big bike ride this morning. Louie has started calling his Christmas present his 'big boy bike', which is funny because he looks even smaller on it than usual, if that's possible!

After they left, I FaceTimed Flora. Georgia from school (and now Oscar's girlfriend again) is having a party at her house on New Year's Eve, and she's invited everyone, including both of us.

'Do you fancy going?' I ask Flora.

'I would love to, Edie, but I think I should stay at home. My mum has been feeling really bad recently.'

Sara, Flora's Mum, has MS (which stands for multiple sclerosis), which is a disease that affects the nervous system. There are different sorts, but in Sara's case it means she gets really ill sometimes and finds it hard to move. Flora is her mum's carer, so she's got to help her a lot more than other daughters help their mums. She does all the washing and cooking and cleaning, and she even helps her mum have a bath.

Over Christmas, Sara caught a cold, which can be quite serious if you have MS. The doctors give her some special drugs for her MS, which affect her immune system – the part of the body that fights illnesses and things like coughs and colds.

When I get a cold, I just get a bit snotty and grumpy, but when Sara gets a cold, it can mean that she's got to stay in bed for a few weeks, and sometimes it gets so bad she has to go to hospital.

'Well, if you're not going, I'm not going. I'd much rather spend it with you.'

'Edie! But all your friends will be there!'

I love all of my friends, but after a really busy Christmas seeing people and doing things, I just want to talk to Flora. When I hang out with her I feel calm and able to be myself.

'I know, but I won't have seen you in eight whole

days, which feels like for ever. We'll have a lot to catch up on!' I say, grinning.

'If you really want to, that would be amazing,' Flora says, and we hang up.

Because the boys are out for most of the day, me and my mum are having a 'girls' day'. We were going to start by having a walk, but I didn't fancy leaving the house, so we've put our pyjamas back on to watch our favourite Christmas films. So far, we've watched *Home Alone*, *Home Alone 2* and now we're about to watch *The Muppet Christmas Carol*.

'This Scrooge won't be as good as you, though!' Mum says, putting her arm around me. She looks happy. 'You were brilliant, Edie. I don't think I've ever been so proud of you!'

I think back to performing the play, and how much I enjoyed it. I can't wait to go back to drama club after Christmas break. If I'm honest, I'm starting to miss Mr Murphy, even though he's the moodiest man on the planet. I'd never admit it to him, but he is a brilliant drama teacher.

I love watching *The Muppet Christmas Carol* even more

than I did last year, now that I know the story a lot more.

At the point when Scrooge meets the Ghost of Christmas Past, I jump up and start performing the lines from the film. It makes my mum laugh, and at the end of the speech she cheers and claps loudly.

'BRAVO! Come here my little actor!'

I jump on to the sofa and hug her tightly. This is the best girls' day ever!

Saturday 11.58pm

IT'S NEW YEAR'S EVE!!!

Flora has made a late-night feast to eat on Sara's bed, and it is brilliant. There are FOUR different kinds of sandwiches (cheese and pickle, tuna, chicken and, my favourite, jam). There are FIVE different kinds of crisps (Mini Cheddars, Cheeselets, pickled onion Monster Munch, cheese puffs and Twiglets. I don't like Twiglets but Sara LOVES them, so that bowl stayed near her, next to her glass of bubbly on her nightstand).

'Let's play a game,' Sara says, clapping her hands in excitement. 'Let's go round and say something we liked doing this year, and something we're looking forward to doing next year. Flora, you go first!'

Flora is halfway through eating a cheese and pickle sandwich and just shrugs. She doesn't like being surprised with questions, and Sara can tell that Flora feels a little embarrassed. She looks at me with her eyebrows raised.

'I'll go first!' I say. I don't know what to say either, but I know that Flora needs some thinking time.

'Erm, OK, well, my favourite thing I did this year was starting school, and making new friends.' I grin at Flora.

The next question is trickier though. What am I looking forward to doing next year? I think about it for a few seconds.

'And next year I am looking forward to writing a lot more!'

I feel this is a good answer, and I really mean it. But then I remember that I had never finished my poem I had started the other day. I feel a bit guilty about that. I know how much my mum thought I would like writing in the book.

'Hmm, and also maybe acting too!'

'Excellent answers, Edie darling!' Sara picks up her glass. 'Well, my favourite thing about this year was watching this one grow up into a brighter and more confident young woman. I love you so much, Floriana Ito!' She clinks her glass on our Coke cans.

Flora turns red and pushes her mum on the arm. 'Mum! You're so embarrassing!' But secretly you can tell she likes it, and that she loves her mum too.

'And next year I am looking forward to eating plenty more Twiglets and drinking loads more prosecco!'

We laugh as Sara shoves a handful of Twiglets in her mouth. Her phone rings. It is Helen Lawson: Sara's best friend and Georgia's mum. Sara chomps her crisps quickly, just in time to answer it, and on the screen we can see about fifteen of her friends who all look like they've had lots of prosecco themselves.

'SARA! WE MISS YOU!'

Sara laughs and tells her friends that she misses them too.

Flora looks at me and whispers, 'It's five to midnight. Shall we go outside and see if we can see any fireworks?'

I pick up a packet of Mini Cheddars and we take as many blankets as we can carry out of the back door and into the garden. We lay them on the grass, so we don't get wet bums.

We sit down next to each other and look up at the sky. 'I felt embarrassed to say it in front of my mum, but my favourite part of this year was definitely meeting you.' Flora gives a little embarrassed laugh when she says it.

'Me too.' I agree, smiling. 'I think you're—'

Suddenly, we hear a crash in the sky. It's a big, brilliant, red firework. It makes me jump, and I spill the Mini Cheddars everywhere. We're both covered in them. Flora laughs and pops one in her mouth. I like that she finds my clumsiness funny.

Flora turns to me. 'Happy New Year, Edie.'

'Happy New Year, Flora.'

I rest my head on Flora's shoulder and she puts her arm around me. I feel so warm and cosy. This year is going to be brilliant.

33

Sunday 11.11am

I always love New Year's Eve, but the next day, New Year's Day, feels scary. It's the first day of a new year, which feels like the first page of a new book. All white and clean and sparkly and anything could happen. Anything is possible. A bit like my notebook, which is basically entirely blank. But I suppose the point of a new year is that it can be a new start, and it's OK to make mistakes as long as you carry on.

So, even though the new year can be scary, I'm going to make some resolutions anyway. Here's my list of New Year's Resolutions:

- Write regularly. Even if you think it's rubbish writing. The fact that you're writing is good.
- Spend time with friends. Hopefully, one day, Oscar and Flora will like each other and we can hang out all together.
- Be a better friend and be there for them when they need me.
- Find out if you prefer acting or writing.

- Ask Flora to be my girlfriend??!!

The last resolution scares me a bit. It seems a bit grown up and serious. But Oscar and Georgia go out, so why shouldn't me and Flora? Thinking about it, should I have asked if she wanted to be my girlfriend last night when we were watching the fireworks?

But what if she doesn't want to be my girlfriend? Maybe I should wait a bit. Do I even want a girlfriend?

Monday 4.30pm

~~The story of the penguin who wanted to go on holiday~~
~~The story of the man who couldn't stop giggling~~
~~The story of the fox who forgot his way home~~
~~The story of the fairy who had no name~~
~~The story of the woman who lived in a crisp factory~~

I give up.

I am trying to write a new story and I don't know if I can. I can write a title, but that's it. After that, my brain goes empty, and then I'm just staring at a boring piece of paper.

A lot of people say 'write about what you know', but I don't really know anything. I only know what it's like to be a twelve-year-old girl with cerebral palsy living by the seaside in Yorkshire. Which is cool, and I love being me, but would other people really want to read about my life?

I think back to how happy I felt when I played Scrooge in the play. *Am I meant to be an actor, more than a writer?*

Wednesday 7.25am

'DIDI, ARE YOU AWAKE?' Louie yells from outside my bedroom door.

Mum has told him not to come into my room and wake me up early, so what he does now is he stands in the hallway and shouts at me until I answer. It's a clever trick. He makes sure he wakes me up, and at the same time, technically, he hasn't come into my room.

'I'm awake *now* Lou. Are you OK?'

Louie peers around my door and gives me a cheeky grin. I can tell that he has an idea.

'Please can we make a den? Please, please, please?'

Making a den is Louie's favourite thing to do. We do it on special days and as this is the last day of the Christmas holidays, it is time!

We sneak downstairs quietly, because Mum and Dad are still fast asleep, taking as many duvets, blankets, pillows and cushions as we can from the airing cupboard and our beds.

In the living room, we arrange the two armchairs back to back, and we drape sheets over them to make a roof.

We cover the den floor with cushions and duvets to make it super-duper comfy.

When it's done, me and Louie get inside and pull down the 'door', which is just another sheet. It is warm and cosy. Louie hugs me.

'I'll miss you when we go back to school, Didi!'

'Me too, Louie! But you'll see me every night after school, so don't worry! Are you looking forward to seeing your friends?'

Louie nods excitedly. 'I am excited to see Ralph, and Harry and Ruby and Martha and Max and Kai!'

I rearrange the cushions on the floor. 'Woah, you have lots of friends!'

'Ralph is my bestest best friend though! Who is your bestest best friend? Oscar?'

I nod.

Louie holds my hand. 'I really, really like den days, Didi, and I really, really like you!'

'I really, really like you too, Louie!' I say, hugging him tightly.

It's the first day back at school after the Christmas holidays and, boy, it's been a struggle. It's been hard to get through the day without constantly eating Christmas snacks. I miss being able to pop my head into the fridge every ten minutes for another mini sausage roll.

It's finally home time and me and Oscar are walking home. He looks as tired as I am. We're walking extra slow, and I cling to Oscar tightly so I don't fall over (because the more tired I am, the more likely I am to fall over).

'Well, Christmas didn't cheer Mr Murphy up! He's still as moody as ever. Cranky McCrankerface!' Oscar says. I haven't seen him all day because he had football practice at lunchtime, so I ate my sandwiches with Georgia. The good part is that I managed to invite Georgia, Chloe and Poppy to mine for a sleepover this weekend. They are all excited!

'Oh, he's not that bad. Mr Murphy's actually a bit of a softie!' I tell Oscar.

'It's all right for you, he likes you because you're so

good at acting! In fact, he likes you so much that he has started calling me "Edie's friend". Oh, and he wanted me to remind you that drama club starts next Thursday.'

I laugh. 'Noted! At least you *have* a tutor, even if he is moody. We've got a different one every week. Today we had Mrs Finchley, who talked to me like I was a baby.'

I kick some brown leaves on the pavement. The truth is that I really miss Mrs Adler. She's my usual tutor but she's away for a bit because she's just had a baby with her wife. Well, two babies actually. Twin girls!

'Are you getting a lift to school tomorrow? It's freezing at the moment,' Oscar says.

I laugh at Oscar. Honestly, I am meant to be the disabled one, but it's usually Oscar who tries to avoid walking or being outside!

'Yeah, Grandad Eric has offered. I'll take him up on it!'

Oscar grins. 'Yes! See ya tomorrow! I hope Grandad

Eric plays that old music by that guy again, what was he called? Stevie something?'

'Stevie Nicks! Stevie is a woman, Osc!'

'Really?' Oscar asks. 'Well, man or woman, I like her! See ya, Edie!'

Oscar runs down the street, clearly trying to keep warm. I watch him until he disappears round the corner.

'You two are gross!' Georgia says, laughing.

She's watching me and Oscar swap our sandwiches, so we have half a jam sandwich, and the other half cheese, and then we mix them both in one big cheesy-jam mess of a sandwich. It's one of our best friend traditions.

Oscar offers her a bite of the jam sandwich, but Georgia shakes her head, as if we're offering her a sandwich made of poo.

'Georgia, just try it! It's nice, honestly!'

Flora walks over and sits on the bench next to me. 'Oh no, are they trying to convince you to eat their weird sandwiches too, Georgia?' Flora asks.

'At least you tried it,' I say, offering my cheese sandwich to Georgia one last time, who bats it away from me. I shrug and turn to Oscar. 'More for us then, mate!'

'How was your morning, Flora?' Georgia asks.

Flora is in the year above us and finding out what she's doing in lessons is like looking into the future and seeing what's ahead of us. So far, what lies ahead just

seems to be a lot more homework and confusing
algebra. Great!

'Really good. Double art!' Flora grins. She doesn't
smile a lot, but when she does, she lights up. 'We had to
paint something we'd done in the holidays so I painted
this.'

She pulls her sketchbook out of her bag and opens it.

'Flora that's seriously amazing. Is that you and Edie?' Oscar asks. Flora nods and I beam.

'I love it so much!' Georgia says, and smacks Oscar playfully on the arm. 'Why don't you paint pictures of us Oscar?'

Oscar snorts. 'Because I'm a properly rubbish artist. Maybe I could get tips from Miss Jamison when I have art. She's such a good teacher! Don't worry, next time I score a goal at football I will dedicate it to you.'

Georgia rolls her eyes sarcastically. 'Lucky me.'

To change the subject, I ask Georgia if she likes painting. She shakes her head. 'The only thing I like painting is my nails!' She holds her hands out to show us her glitter manicure. 'We could do nails at our sleepover this weekend!'

Georgia is really pretty. She curls her hair every morning before school because she likes it better that way. It's such dedication!

'Actually,' Georgia says, 'I've been thinking about trying acting. You were amazing in the Christmas play. It looked fun and I wondered if you'd mind if I came to drama club with you?'

'Georgia, I would love that!' I say. I think she would be brilliant at acting. 'We start back next Thursday. Come with me and I'll introduce you to everybody!'

'I'm coming too,' Flora says, opening her lunchbox and popping a grape in her mouth. 'Mr Murphy says I can come and help do the sets for his GCSE class, even though we're not rehearsing for a play.'

YES!!! Brilliant with a capital B. I was so sad Flora wouldn't be at drama club any more, because there's no need for a set designer. She really made it feel complete last term!

Oscar looks properly moody. 'Great,' he whines, shoving the last bit of his sandwich into his mouth. 'So am I the only person who isn't going to drama club?'

'You don't need to feel left out,' I say. 'You can join too, Osc.'

'And spend even more time with Moody Murphy? No thank you. I'll stick to football!' He gets up and pretends to score a goal.

Saturday 9.01pm

We're all in my bedroom, after dinner. Flora couldn't come because she is looking after Sara, which is a shame – but I hope there will be more times for her to join in the fun.

'Edie, I can't believe I haven't seen you since the Christmas play! How have you been?' Poppy asks, painting her toenails and sitting on the beanbag.

Poppy bringing up the Christmas play made me realise that I hadn't told the girls about what had happened *after* the play. The girls always talk about boys, so why shouldn't I tell them about Flora?

'Thanks. Well, erm, actually,' I start. I suddenly feel nervous but I don't know why. 'After the play, Flora kissed me . . . on the lips.'

'Did you want her to kiss you?' Georgia asks.

'Yes,' I grin. 'Yes I did!'

Georgia, Poppy and Chloe grin too.

'So, what now?' Chloe asks.

'Are you girlfriend and girlfriend?' Georgia asks, turning to face me on the bed. 'Would you say you were gay, or what?'

Those are a lot of questions. I *think* I want Flora to be my girlfriend, but I'm not sure whether she wants to be. It all seems quite grown up and I like being friends. What if being a girlfriend changes things?

I take a deep breath.

'I just know I enjoyed our kiss, and my tummy feels funny when we're together, and I really like talking to her, and that she's one of my favourite people to hang out with.'

'That sounds brilliant, Edie!' Georgia says. 'I'm happy for you!'

There's a knock on my door. Dad comes in, carrying four mugs of hot chocolate, and Louie follows him with a jar of marshmallows.

'Who wants MALLOWS?' Louie screams at the top of his voice.

We shout, 'YES PLEASE!'

Louie pokes his tongue out in concentration and goes up to each of us in turn, counting out five marshmallows each to make sure everybody gets their fair share.

After he gives Poppy her five, she kisses him on the cheek and says, 'Thank you, Lou!'

Louie goes bright red. Then he looks at my dad and runs straight out of the room.

Dad chuckles, shakes his head and turns to leave my room. 'Night, girls!'

'Night night, Mr Eckhart.'

When he shuts the door, Georgia, Poppy and Chloe lift up their hot chocolates to toast. 'To Edie and Flora!'

I smile and I 'cheers' my friends. But it is my turn to go red.

Midnight

My friend Chloe is awesome – but she's such a loud snorer! She's one of the smallest people in our year but when she's asleep, she makes the same sound as a gigantic hippopotamus!

I put my head under my pillow and I try to sleep, but for some reason I can't.

I think back to Georgia's question earlier in the evening: 'Would you say you were gay, or what?'

Even though 'gay' is only a three letter word, it feels like a pretty BIG word. I don't know if that word describes me. Just because I kissed one girl, does that make me gay? The girls asked me a lot of questions tonight and, if I'm honest, I don't really know any of the answers.

Sunday 3pm

I'm having such a lovely Sunday. This morning after the girls left, I went swimming with my dad and Louie. I still find swimming difficult, but I am definitely improving. My dad says it's 'all in the breathing', but I am not totally sure what that means. All I can do is keep trying, going to the pool regularly, and we'll get there.

In the afternoon, I went for a walk on the beach with Flora. We pointed whenever we saw a dog we liked. I think between us we pointed at every dog! Flora's favourites are the big dogs, like the Labradors and the Dalmatians, and I like the smaller cute, furry dogs – all the ones that look like teddy bears.

Finally, we made it to 'our bench', which is a spot overlooking the sea where Flora and I would sit and talk when we were getting to know each other last year. I can't imagine ever not knowing Flora now; it feels like I've known her for ever!

It is the perfect spot to ask Flora to be my girlfriend! I like her lots, and I love spending time with her, so I think I should ask her, shouldn't I? Why not? Georgia definitely would if she was in my position. I swallow a few times, suddenly feeling nervous.

'Are you OK, Edie? What's wrong?' Flora asks, looking worried.

'Oh, no, nothing.' I shrug. 'Just thinking about school.'

Tuesday 10.02am – English Class

Our English teacher, Mr Messer, is brilliant, and is now my second favourite teacher of all time (behind Mrs Adler, obvs). Mr Messer always wears bright jumpers that look super soft. Today he is wearing a purple jumper.

He's new to the school this term, and has replaced my old English teacher, Mrs Brown, who was a bit boring . . . I fell asleep in two of her lessons!

Mr Messer is very tall and thin, and he's got the deepest voice I've ever heard. Much deeper than my dad's voice, and even deeper than Grandad Eric's.

When he started at the school last week, he seemed quite nervous and would talk so quietly we could hardly hear him. But today he seems to have got over his fear of talking. He's actually surprisingly funny.

His desk is always covered in paper, so our class has started to call him 'Mr Messy'. When he heard that we called him that, he frowned, but admitted that the nickname was extremely accurate!

I sit next to my friend Pip. I know her through Georgia, but now that I sit next to her in English we've

53

got a lot closer. She always seems confident and grown up, like she has all of the answers, and she already knows that she wants to be a vet when she's older.

'Morning, gang!' Mr Messer says from the front of the class. He's already written a question on the whiteboard. 'Take your seats. As you might have spotted, we're focusing on one BIG question for today's lesson: Who am I?'

The class giggles, and we look around at each other. *Is Mr Messer having a funny five minutes and forgotten who he is?*

Pip is the brave one in our class. She puts her hand up.

'You're Mr Messer. Our English teacher, sir.' Pip tells him.

He puts his hands on his hips triumphantly and says, 'That's right! I am Mr Messer!'

Then he draws an arrow off the question and next to it writes 'Mr Messer – English teacher'.

He turns back to face us. 'But to some people I am "Tim".'

He draws another arrow with 'Tim' next to it. The

class giggles a bit. I always forget that teachers have first names. It's weird to think that they're actual people sometimes.

'Well, if you're laughing at "Tim", you're definitely going to laugh at what my girlfriend calls me,' he admits, drawing an arrow and jotting down "Pookie".'

The whole class laughs, and me and Pip properly get the giggles. Mr Messer grumbles and laughs at the same time. 'I hate that one, but when I say that she just calls me it more.'

He starts writing more:

'Mr Messy' – the name we call him.

'Timothy' – the name his mum calls him.

'Shrek' – the name his rugby team call him because his ears stick out. *That's a bit of a mean one!*

'The Beanpole' – the name his friends call him, because he's so tall.

'Uncle Tim' – the name his niece calls him.

He fills the entire board with other

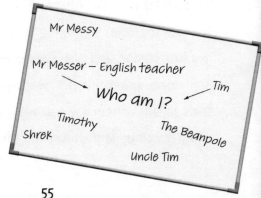

descriptions. 'Teacher', 'boyfriend', 'son', 'uncle', 'rugby player', 'wine drinker', 'book lover', 'marathon runner', 'gamer'.

It was funny to think that one person can be so many things.

'Now open your books. It's your turn. Who are you? You can start with nicknames, and names people use to describe you, but I want you to go further than that. I want you to use this as an exercise to explore who you are NOW, but also who you want to be in the future. Off you go. You can use different coloured pens for present you and future you. It should be fun!'

Everybody starts scribbling away in their exercise journals, but I hesitate slightly.

Eventually, I write down 'Didi', which is what Louie calls me, and 'mushroom' because Mum calls me that, but then I don't know what else to write. Everybody else just calls me 'Edie'.

I look around, and everybody else seems to have their head down, writing loads. I look at Pip's page. Oh no! She's already written down about twenty different things. I look up at the board. Mr Messer wrote 'boyfriend' – I wish I could write 'girlfriend', that would fill up a little section at least. And what DO I want to be when I'm older? Maybe I should write actor, but I can't be completely sure. I haven't even tried it this year; I might be terrible after a long break. And if I can't write in this journal, then how on earth am I supposed to be a writer. I must have lost my spark.

Maybe I should write 'best friend' but then I remember Oscar being funny about Flora the other day and it makes me question that too. Are we becoming less close? Can I still say that me and Oscar are best friends? I'm not sure any more. I feel a lump in my throat.

'OK, Edie?' Mr Messer asks. He must've seen me looking around at everybody. I nod, and put my head down.

I eventually copy Mr Messer's 'book lover' description because at least that is true. And I put 'sausage roll fanatic' and 'likes Marvel movies'. But I don't write anything else for the rest of the lesson. I just pretend by moving my pen across the page with the lid still on.

When the bell goes at the end of class, I feel relieved.

'OK, for homework I want you to take the collection of names and descriptions you have written to spark the next step. I want you all to do a presentation for the class next week – on *you*. This will go towards your speaking and listening grade for this year. This is extremely important because it counts towards your overall grade at the end of the year. I hope you spend the time on it, because it really matters what you create and present to the class. Give it your all! Be creative, surprise me and bring props, but above all, tell me who you really are.' Mr Messer's eyes are shining. 'And even what you want to be when this school is nothing but a distant memory!'

This is the worst homework ever! I feel a thick lump in my throat. How can I stand up in front of my class and tell them who I am when I don't even know? I can't make a whole presentation about how my brother can't properly pronounce my name and how my mum calls me 'mushroom', can I?

At least I have a week to think about what to say. Hopefully before then I can work out who I actually am!

It is the first drama club back, and we are all pretending to be small creatures.

I've decided to be a snail. I figured that I am already quite slow, so I might as well choose the slowest animal! I look over at Georgia to make sure she's OK – it's always tough being the new one in a group.

She's flapping her arms, weaving in and out of the group pretending to be a butterfly, and she's got the biggest smile on her face. I can tell she's enjoying it.

The loudest animal is Tom. He's decided to be a bee, and whenever somebody gets close to him, he buzzes loudly and chases them around the hall. It's so funny.

Poppy is sliding around on the floor next to me, slithering slowly closer and closer. I think she's pretending to be a worm or snake.

'Great work, everyone. And relax,' Mr Murphy commands. 'For those of you not already on the floor, please sit down and form a circle.'

Georgia runs over and shuffles in between me and Poppy.

'Firstly,' Mr Murphy booms, 'I need to say how brilliant the Christmas play was. From the set design,' Mr Murphy points to Flora, who is busy painting a boat on some wood panelling for another drama project, 'to our very own female Scrooge.' Everyone claps.

'I also want to welcome Georgia to the group. Everyone give Georgia a round of applause.'

Georgia giggles and I put my arm around her.

'Now, for this term,' Mr Murphy beams, 'I really want to push you as actors, as performers and as people. For that reason, I am pleased to announce we all have the opportunity to go on a drama trip at half-term to Rosedale in North Yorkshire. With your parents' or guardians' permission, of course.'

An actual trip! That'll be brilliant. I really hope Mum and Dad let me go!

Mr Murphy explains that it will be a 'drama

bootcamp', where we will 'hone our dramatic skills'. At
the end of the week, we will put on a show for our
friends and family.

'You are all used to each other by now,' he went on,
'which means you're comfortable. But the best actors are
pushed outside their comfort zones once in a while. For
that reason, we'll be going with another school. It will be
a great chance to learn new skills, and make some new
friends too!'

☆☆☆

'And we get to "hone our dramatic skills" Mr Murphy
says, although I don't really know what that means.
Anyway, pleaaaaaase can I go?' I clasp my hands together
pleadingly.

'You'd be away for *all* of half-term? I thought we
could go camping. It feels like ages since our last trip,'
my dad says, looking a bit disappointed and taking
another bite of his lasagne.

'And you've never been away from us for that long
before. I don't know if you're ready,' Mum admits,

looking between me and Dad.

I'm not even touching my lasagne until I know I can go. I take a deep breath. 'Yes, it is scary, but I have lots of friends going too. I have Georgia and Poppy, and even Flora is coming. Mr Murphy will be there and the teacher from the other school. And because it is half-term, we're allowed to take our phones, so if anything happens or I need you, I can just ring you and you can come and get me. Plus it'd be great for me to establish my independence and do things with my classmates. If you don't let me go, it's because I'm disabled, and you know that isn't fair!'

Mum raises an eyebrow. 'You planned that speech, didn't you?'

I smile and nod sheepishly. 'Did it work?'

Dad gives Mum a look. 'Our girl's got a point, love.'

'OK, Edie love, you can go!'

I hug them both so hard.

I AM GOING ON A TRIP!

Monday 1.32pm – Lunchtime

'Edie, stop wriggling and go to the toilet!' Oscar tells me.

'How do you know I need a wee?' I ask him from my spot on the bench.

'Because you won't stop moving around!' Flora laughs.

Of course they're both right.

Flora and Oscar know me so well, they know that I need to go to the loo IMMEDIATELY. But if I'm honest, I am nervous about going to the toilet and leaving Oscar and Flora alone together. What if they don't get on? What if they have an argument?

Even though this worries me, I need to go and have a wee. I suddenly have a great idea.

'Well, I'd better go to the loo,' I wriggle to my feet. 'Hey, don't you both like football? You could talk about that when I'm gone.'

I walk as quickly as I can to the toilet.

When I come back to the courtyard I can't believe what I am seeing. Oscar and Flora are *laughing* together. Are Flora and Oscar *really* getting on?

'What are you two talking about?' I ask them.

'Football – like you suggested! We're trying to see how much it would cost us to tempt Mo Salah to come and play for Bridlington Town,' Oscar says, still laughing.

'Who's Mo Wotsit? Is he one of the good players

 then?' I ask, trying to get in on the joke. I don't get football.

This makes Flora and Oscar laugh even more. This makes me feel silly, but I am determined to join in with the conversation.

'Well, if you both think he's good, he must be. I only know Gary Lineker, and that's mainly because he's the crisp man.'

Oscar and Flora both laugh EVEN MORE. Phew. I might not know anything about football, but at least I can still make them both laugh.

At last, they finish talking about footie and Oscar takes his rubbish to the bin.

'Have you finished your English homework then?

Have you finally figured out "who you are"?' Flora asks.

I had told her earlier about the homework Mr Messer gave us. Flora's advice was to stop overthinking it and to just write something from the heart.

Who am I? How can three words feel like such a big question? I have put the homework off and off and off, every single day, and now it is due tomorrow and I still haven't written anything for it.

'Yep! All done!' I say cheerfully.

I think it's the first time I have ever properly lied to Flora and I feel terrible for it, but it's better than telling the truth: that I haven't done it because I don't know who I am. Which means maybe my friends don't know either.

Tuesday 10.01am – AKA DEADLINE DAY

I feel sick. I walk into the classroom, certain that I already look suspicious. I always say hello to Mr Messer, but this time I don't. I'm afraid that if I look at him in the eye, he'll know immediately that I haven't done my homework.

'Morning, Edie. Are you OK?' Mr Messer asks, sounding a bit concerned.

I still don't look at him as I say, 'Fine thanks, sir', trying to sound as cool and as calm as possible, but my voice quivers a little bit.

More people come into the classroom, and I am relieved to see Pip. She always cheers me up. But then she starts getting out her homework. She has different bits of coloured paper, and all of it is covered in *glitter*!

I look around the class. Noah Long even has a microphone and a little keyboard. Is he going to sing a song about who he is?

The lump in my throat is so thick now, I can barely swallow.

I try to think about all the things I could do to avoid getting in trouble. Could I use 'the Card'?

The Card is when Oscar and I use my disability as an excuse to get out of something we really don't want to do. We can't use it every  day, because people would get suspicious, but, every now and then, it can be extremely useful.

I think about using the Card and using my cerebral palsy as an excuse for not doing the homework. For example, I could I say that I *had* finished my presentation, but on the way to school I fell, and the whole presentation landed in a big puddle, and then a dog ate it.

'Morning, class! Right, the day is here.' Mr Messer excitedly claps his hands together. 'Your presentations. We might not get through you all today, but anybody we don't get to, we can see your brilliant work tomorrow.'

HOPE! Maybe, just maybe, he won't pick me today, and then tonight I can go home and figure out what to say. Even that plan doesn't fill me with much confidence though. If I haven't figured it out in the past week, I don't know if an extra day will help.

'Starting with . . . ah, Pip!'

Pip is thrilled to be chosen first. She picks up her sparkly paper and practically jogs to the front of the class.

'Hello, I am Pip, and I am a future vet.'

Pip reveals a big, brilliant picture printed on cardboard, of herself, dressed as a vet, surrounded by loads of different animals. It's impressive and makes me feel more nervous. After that, I don't hear a lot of Pip's presentation. I am too busy thinking about how to get out of the classroom, and fast. Should I say that I need the loo? All of the teachers know that when I need a wee, I absolutely need to go. It could be the perfect excuse. I can go and hide in the bathrooms for the rest of the lesson.

The class starts clapping and I am snapped back into reality. Pip, beaming, sits back next to me. 'Well done,' I whisper.

'And now let's have Edie!' Mr Murphy says.

Everything stops for a second, but at the same time my brain feels like it's whirring at a million miles a second. My breathing gets faster and my palms feel sweaty. The classroom blurs, as I realise that the only thing I can say at this point to Mr Messer is the truth.

'I haven't done it, sir.'

Everyone looks at me. Mr Messer's eyes are wide. I wonder if he's going to shout at me, or send me out, or even make me go to the headteacher's office. I feel myself go bright red.

'Why not, Edie?' Mr Messer asks calmly. This upsets me more than if he shouted.

I know that if I said anything else, I would cry, so instead I just shrug my shoulders.

'That's disappointing, Edie. Wait after class. Now let's have, er, Noah! And have you brought a keyboard? Fancy!'

The whole class turns to watch Noah, who raps his

presentation while playing keyboard, and I am relieved that they are no longer looking at me.

The minutes drag on, and more people present to the class. I know that class is nearly over. I don't know what Mr Messer is going to say to me but I know that it won't be good.

When the bell rings, my stomach drops. Everybody else packs up their stuff and leaves the classroom, and I stay sitting down, looking at my desk. Before she goes, Pip gives me a sympathetic smile.

When there's nobody else in the room, Mr Messer walks over to me and sits in Pip's seat.

He doesn't shout, he just quietly asks, 'So, Edie, why didn't you do the homework?'

I still don't want to cry in front of him, so I say nothing.

He leans back in his chair. 'Look, Edie, if there's something the matter, or a reason why you couldn't, or didn't want to do the work, I'd rather you talked to me.'

How could I tell him that I didn't do the homework because I have no idea who I am or what I want to be? I feel like a complete and utter fool. It's so embarrassing!

Mr Messer sighs heavily. 'Edie,' he says gently, 'if you won't talk to me, I'll have no choice but to give you a detention and I really don't want to do that. Up until now you've been a delight to teach. This is so unlike you.'

I don't say anything. Mr Messer stands up and walks back to his desk.

'Come back here lunchtime tomorrow for your detention. I'm sorry, Edie, but you left me no choice.'

DETENTION SLIP

Name: Edie

Day: Wednesday

Room:

He comes back and hands me a piece of paper.

I feel ashamed. Without looking at Mr Messer I leave the room and I head to the loos.

Once I'm in the toilet cubicle and I know that nobody can hear me, I cry and I cry and I cry.

Tuesday lunchtime

'YOU? Have a detention?' Oscar exclaimed when I told him why I couldn't have lunch with him. 'Why? What did you do?'

Oscar still couldn't believe it. We'd known each other for eight years and in all that time I had never got into trouble. Sometimes at primary school, if I was chatting to Oscar loads, or being loud and excitable, I would get a stern 'shhh!' from the teacher, but that would be it. That would be enough for me to be quiet, put my head down and get on with my work.

Never had I EVER got a detention before now.

Oscar promised me he wouldn't tell my parents (or *his* parents, because they would probably just blab to mine).

4pm

When I get home, Mum is waiting for me in the kitchen, looking stern. She held her phone up. 'Edie? A *detention*?'

The school have clearly informed Mum via text message.

'I'm sorry, Mum. It won't happen again,' is all I could say as I sit opposite her at the table.

Mum puts her hand on mine.

'Mr Messer told me that you hadn't done your homework and couldn't give him a reason why. Edie, what's wrong? You can talk to me.'

Like earlier with Mr Messer, I didn't want to admit that I didn't know how to even start the presentation.

'I'm not angry with you about not doing your homework, but I am upset that you feel as if you can't talk to me.'

I don't know what to do or say, so instead I stay silent.

'Edie, I've got no choice but to ground you unless you tell me what is going on.'

I pull my hand away
from Mum's, cross my arms
and press my lips together as if
they're zipped shut.

'You're grounded this weekend, Edie.'

Thursday 6.59pm

OSCAR

Do you want to come over and bake
cakes for Mum's birthday tomorrow?

I'm grounded 😞

OSCAR

What? ALL WEEKEND???

Jeez, you didn't do one piece of homework!
Imagine if you did something actually bad! 😂

I laugh at the text from Oscar and put my phone down
on my bed. This is lits the worst January ever. I thought
this term would be absolutely brilliant but so far it's
properly rubbish. The only thing to look forward to now
is the drama trip. My parents said I can still go to that
at least.

'Knock, knock,' Dad says, coming into my room.
'Only me!'

He sits on my bed but faces away, like he does when he wants to have a serious conversation but pretends it's a casual chat.

'Your mum tells me that you don't want to talk about the homework thing.'

I sigh and shake my head, and my bottom lip shakes a little bit. I feel like I could cry any second.

'Well, if you'd rather be locked up in our house hanging out with us than tell us what the matter is, it must be serious.' I try and smile.

He continues, 'I just hope you know that if and when you're ready to talk, me and your mum are always there for you. We're proud of you. We want you to feel like you can confide in us, so whenever you're ready . . .'

I nod. 'I know, Dad. I love you.'

We go downstairs for tea, and we don't talk about it again.

After Oscar invited me to bake cakes, Georgia and Chloe invited me to go shopping. But I can't do that either.

To make things worse, I'm not even allowed to stay in my bedroom and mind my own business, like people who are grounded on telly do. Instead, I've had to come with my mum to a birthday party of a boy in Louie's class and tomorrow I have to go car shopping with my dad. Boring with a capital B.

I'm sitting at the party with my mum and all the other mums, and they're chatting about 'the efficiency of electric cars'. I can't believe it. I don't do one tiny bit of homework and this is how I get punished. I feel myself getting angry. I imagine Georgia and Chloe at the shopping centre without me. They are probably getting milkshakes right now.

To kill a bit of time, I get up to pour myself a cup of squash from the buffet table. I put two plastic cups together, one inside the other, and smile. It reminds me of the first time I met Flora. She taught me the 'two cups together' trick, to make sure the plastic doesn't break and it's sturdier so there's less spillages.

Suddenly, I hear Louie's voice, followed by another boy's cries.

Mum gets up off her chair and rushes up to Louie.

'What's happened?'

'He hit me!' a boy with curly ginger hair says, pointing at Louie.

Louie hit somebody? I don't think so!

Mum talks to the boy and the other mum and she tries to make Louie apologise. But he refuses to say sorry, so she grabs Louie by the wrist and pulls him towards me at the table.

'Edie, we're leaving.' I follow them both out, but take the squash for the road.

In the car, it is completely silent for a while. Mum doesn't even put the radio on.

'Hitting a boy, Louie! Whyever would you do that?' Mum asks him, looking at us in her rear-view mirror.

Louie looks at me and bursts out crying. Between sobs he manages to say, 'He . . . said . . . that Edie . . . had a . . . funny walk.'

Louie hit someone *because of me*?

Mum says quietly, 'And is that why you hit him?'

Louie's bottom lip sticks out even further. He cries even louder.

To cheer Louie up, I say, 'To be fair, I *do* have a funny walk!'

Louie shakes his head hard. 'No you don't! It's your walk, and I like it.'

My heart feels like it could burst into a million pieces.

My mum softens. 'Oh, Louie love, sometimes there will be people who are mean about Edie, because she's a bit different, but you can't go around hitting everybody who says anything nasty.'

'Yes I can!' Louie says firmly. 'I'm a boxer, just like Grandad Eric!'

Mum snorts. 'Grandad Eric isn't a boxer, he couldn't even hit a teddy bear.'

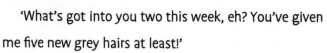

We all laugh, and then Mum sighs.

'What's got into you two this week, eh? You've given me five new grey hairs at least!'

'Sorry, Mum,' we mumble.

Louie looks at me with his big brown eyes. 'I love you, Didi, especially your walk.'

I smile at my little brother and I squeeze his hand tightly. I don't think there's anybody I love more than him in the entire world.

Sunday 8.25am

> **Good luck at football today! X**

FLORA

> Thanks ☺ I'm really going to miss you xxx

'Dad, it's Flora's first football match of the year and everybody's going. Oscar's going, Chloe's going, Georgia's going, Poppy's—'

Dad interrupts me, taking a slurp of his tea. 'You're listing all these people like I should care! Edie, you're grounded today.'

I slump back down on the kitchen chair and Louie runs into the room holding a toy rocket.

Dad stands up. 'You too, Rocky, put your shoes on. If my kids insist on rebelling, then they're spending the day traipsing around every car showroom in this town until I find the most eco-friendly machine in all the land. Think of it as a quest!'

Seriously rubbish quest, if you ask me. I'd rather be in biology, and that's saying something.

Monday 6.48pm

'Edie love, I don't think I've ever been more proud of you!' Grandad Eric beams from the dinner table. 'I got plenty of detentions in my day. And the ruler. And the slipper. Never did me any harm, did it?'

'Dad!' Mum shouts at him. It always makes me laugh that even though Mum is Grandad Eric's daughter, it is always her shouting at him!

'Were you allowed to wear your slippers to school Grandad?' Louie asks him, raising one eyebrow in confusion.

'No, lad, they'd smack your bum with it if you were naughty.'

Mum changes the subject. 'Have you sorted out your hospital appointment yet? For your stomach pain?'

Grandad Eric waves his hand, as if he is physically batting away the question. 'Angela love, stop fussing and pass me the gravy.' He winks at me. 'Rebels together, you and me!'

For the first time in days I don't feel bad about getting that detention.

Sunday 2.02pm

'Edie, it feels like you've been grounded for ever!' Oscar
cheers when he gets to my house. 'I'm so glad I can see
you again!' He hugs me.

'Osc,' I laugh, 'it's lits been a weekend!'

'Yeah, but I really fancied you
making cakes with me and having
a lazy day watching movies and
eating chocolate.'

I have to admit that I missed
Oscar the most at the weekend. He is my forever
friend, and the person that I don't need to do anything
with for us to be friends. Even when he just comes to my
house and we sit together, we have a brilliant time.

'Ah, that would have been so nice. How was your
mum's birthday?'

'Really fun!' Oscar grins. 'My mum seemed to have a
nice time. We all made pizzas and I've discovered the
best topping combo ever . . . anchovies, olives and
capers.'

I pull a face at him and shiver in disgust. 'Gross. That

sounds properly disgusting.'

Oscar shrugs, throws a Skittle up in the air and tries to catch it in his mouth, but instead it hits his cheek and falls on the floor.

He picks it up quickly. 'Five second rule!' He chews and pulls a funny face. 'Mmm, hairy.'

I laugh at him, and I am so glad I am no longer grounded.

'We missed you at the football on Sunday. Flora was so good. She delivered a hat-trick of assists!' Oscar says excitedly.

I have no idea what that means, so I just say, 'Great! We all love a hat-trick of assists, it's like my favourite thing ever, and just good, all-round football work!' and I hope Oscar doesn't think I'm silly for not knowing anything about football.

'Edie,' Oscar says, frowning slightly, 'you don't need to talk about football just because me and Flora like football.'

'But I got excited that you two were getting on, and I wanted to join in,' I admit. 'I thought if I liked football too, then we could all hang out and it could be easier. I hated how awkward that was.'

'It's not up to you to make sure that me and Flora get on or have stuff to talk about. All that matters is that you like us both.'

'Yeah, but I would love it if we could all hang out, like a big gang.'

'We do, Edie, stop worrying! I like Flora, I do. I mean, I'm a bit annoyed that she's better at football than I am, but I guess in time I'll get over that.'

I laugh.

'You don't need to fix everyone and make people happy. Just do things that make *you* happy. And it's OK not to have all of the answers yet. And, by the way, I meant what I said – I *do* really like Flora. I just find it weird that you hang out with somebody who isn't me as much as you do. It used to be you and me against the world.'

I felt the same way when Oscar started going out with Georgia. A sort of jealous feeling.

'It's not because Flora is another girl either,' Osc quickly blurts out. 'I think it's cool that you're gay, or whatever.'

For the first time since Christmas, I feel like I am able to be honest, even though I am a bit worried he might laugh at me. 'I don't know if I *am* gay, Oscar,' I admit. 'And Flora isn't my girlfriend. I don't know whether she would want to be my girlfriend. I don't know whether *I* want her to be my girlfriend. I have a lot of questions in my head right now that I don't know the answers to. Which is scary.'

I look down at the floor. I feel embarrassed saying all of these things out loud.

'I feel the same way, Edie mate. There's a lot of stuff that I don't know the answer to either. And there must be loads more questions in your head with your disability, and now how you feel about Flora.'

I nod. I feel so relieved that he understands. I feel much freer now I've told him. I can't believe I was worried that he might think I was being silly.

'How do you feel about Flora, though? Do you like her – I mean, like her in a more–than-friends way?' he asks.

I nod, and I can't help but smile. 'I really like her, Oscar. She's funny and kind and such a brilliant artist! I don't know whether I am gay or not, or what *more-than-*

friends means, but I *do* know that I really like holding her hand.'

Oscar eats a handful of Skittles. 'That sounds brilliant, Edie, but just so you know, when we're grown up, I have dibs on marrying Black Widow. I don't care if you fancy girls, you're not having my lady!'

'I'll fight you for her.' I put up my fists in a pretend fight, and Oscar hits me playfully with the cushion.

This is a great Sunday.

Monday 2.02pm

I'm running to my English class and I am already very, very late.

I blame Oscar, Flora and Georgia. We were outside having lunch and laughing about Oscar's weird second toe. It's longer than his big toe and I don't think that's normal. Flora's toe is like mine. Oscar swears that if your second toe is longer than your big toe, like his, it's a sign of intelligence.

'You think you're more intelligent than us? Just because you have a massive toe? Oscar, you're speaking rubbish!' I told him.

'I'm not! Georgia, what's your toe like?' Oscar asked, putting his bare foot in Georgia's face.

Georgia pulled away from his foot, giggling. 'Take your stinky foot away from me. I am not getting my foot out in February, you bunch of absolute weirdos. Anyway, the bell's gone, we need to go to class.'

How had we not heard the bell go? Probably because

we were laughing about our toes. We are weirdos and I love it!

Flora and Oscar quickly put their socks and shoes back on and Oscar helped me with my shoe.

'Shall I walk you to class, Edie?' Oscar asked, but I shook my head. That would make him late for his class.

'I should be fine, Oscar. See you all tonight,' I yelled cheerfully, and off I went. I didn't want them to know how nervous I am about being late for class.

It would be fine normally, but because it's Mr Messer I am doubly nervous. He's already given me a detention; I don't want him to give me another one. He's *really* going to hate me now.

I am so busy walking as fast as I can, I don't see the 'Wet Floor' sign in the corridor. I slip and I fall.

Ow! I land and hear my trousers tear a little bit. I look at my knees. My left knee is bleeding. I think about going to the nurse's office, but I don't want to be even later for Mr Messer. And I don't want him to feel sorry for me either, so I just head to class.

When I get to the classroom, everybody is still unpacking their bags and sitting down. Mr Messer doesn't even notice I am late.

'Are you OK?' Pip asks me, noticing a little bit of blood on my hands.

I nod, feeling embarrassed.

Remind me NEVER to get my toes out at lunchtime ever again.

Thursday 4.58pm – DRAMA

We're playing a game where the group has to describe somebody using one word, phrase or expression. So far, we have described Georgia (I chose to describe her as 'thoughtful', because of all the times she's been there for me and listened) and we described Tom (I chose the word 'joker', because he is always the one who makes the group laugh the most).

I'm nervous, because I don't know how the group will describe me. I don't know how I would describe myself if I had to. I think I would probably use the word 'wobbly'.

'No need to look so nervous, Edie,' Mr Murphy says. 'I'll go first. Talented.'

Flora, who has had her headphones on and has had her back to the group, painting away until now, shouts 'Brilliantly weird'. I laugh, thinking about our strange sandwiches and our toe chat.

After hearing all the ways people describe me, I feel relieved and lighter. It's funny how nobody mentioned my disability. It is definitely part of me, but it doesn't need to be all of me.

I grin, and we move on to the next person in the circle.

☆☆☆

At the end of drama class, we hand over the remaining money-slips for the drama trip. We're leaving on Monday and I can't believe it's nearly here! I am so excited. Everybody is going: Poppy, Georgia, Chloe, Poppy's boyfriend Tom, and even Flora.

I had to persuade Flora. She wanted to stay at home to look after her mum, but Sara told her that she should go and have fun. She also told Flora to stop using her as an excuse not to go out and live a little.

I have noticed this about Flora too. Sometimes she says, 'I can't go there, because I need to look after Mum,' when, actually, I think it's because she wants to be on her own, in her house, quietly drawing away. Flora is definitely an introvert. I think this is why we get on; we're so different but similar at the same time. Why didn't I think of 'extrovert' for my presentation? That one is a no brainer!

Friday 7.25pm

'Happy Start of Half-Term Break!' Mum announces, pulling out a massive golden chicken pie from the oven. It's one of my favourite things she makes, especially when she makes it with peas, carrots, mash and lots and lots of gravy.

Oscar has come round for tea and Louie's best friend Ralph is here too. I really like Ralph. He has a lisp, and floppy blond hair, and he calls me 'Didi' too, because Louie does.

Dad is working a shift at the hospital, so Mum puts his corner of the pie in a Tupperware box. The crispiest bit, because he loves crispy food.

'What are you going to do during half-term, Oscar?' Mum asks.

Oscar shrugs. 'It's going to be properly rubbish. Edie's going on the drama trip, Flora's going, even Georgia's going! Who will I hang out with?'

Louie puts his little hand on Oscar's arm. 'You can come and play with me and Ralph on Monday, Oscar. We're going to Adventureland!'

Ralph nods seriously. 'And you can play Lego with us. If you like Lego. But if you don't like Lego, you don't have to play Lego with us.'

Bless them. I laugh at the thought of Oscar spending his week with two four-year-olds. To be fair, I think he'd have a lovely time!

Oscar grins at them. 'Thanks, Louie! And thanks, Ralph! I do like Lego, but I think I'm going to spend the week playing football.'

I roll my eyes. He's obsessed.

'I went to football once, my daddy took me,' Ralph announces.

'Did you like it?' Oscar asks him.

'Nah. But I did like the chips and Coke we got in the breaky bit.' Ralph shoves a big bit of mash into his mouth.

I like Ralph. He's a boy after my own heart!

Sunday 1.58pm

We've come to York to buy some new clothes for the
school trip.

'You're going to be camping in tents, so you're going
to need a lot of warm clothes for the week. And let's buy
you a big bag to fit everything you need,' my dad says.

I pick a gigantic orange backpack that is
nearly bigger than me and a red
sleeping bag with a hood attached
to it. I think I'm going to be
super cosy in it, and now I'm
even more excited for the trip.

Afterwards, when we've
bought all my bits and bobs, we go to an amazing
restaurant for lunch.

Every section of the restaurant has a different type of
food! Pizza, pasta, curries, Chinese food, noodles,
sushi . . . every time I turn my head I see a different dish I
want to try. This is Amazing with a capital A!

Louie's already big eyes widen even further. 'Can I eat
anything? From any counter?'

I have to admit, I'm as excited as him. I've lits never been anywhere like this before.

Where do I even start? Shall I start with tapas, and then work my way up to every different type of pasta, and then finish with a curry? Or do I mix it up, and do I put noodles on my pizza? I've never done that before.

'Come on, Edie.' My dad offers me his arm and we walk towards the food. 'What do you fancy eating first?'

We both look at each other and head straight for the curry table.

When we're there, I point at the food I want, and Dad scoops the curry, rice, poppadom's and bhajis on to my plate. It all looks delicious. Dad does the same for himself, and we head back.

My mum and Louie get back to our table at the same time, with a paella for Mum and a margherita pizza for Louie. I laugh.

'All this choice, Lou, and you *still* go for a margherita pizza? You were so excited about the options a moment ago.'

Louie nods enthusiastically. 'I just love margherita pizza!'

I eat my curry. I remember back to telling Mum that 'it'll be great for me to establish my independence' but now the trip is coming up, I worry that I'm not old enough to be independent for five whole days.

I think Mum has a sort of sixth sense, because whenever something worries me, she can always tell.

'Are you OK, Edie?'

I hesitate. If I tell her that I'm worried about the trip, will she stop me going? Either way, it would make me feel better to talk about it, so I pop my fork on the table and I take a deep breath.

'I'm worried I won't be able to cope on the school trip. Five days is a *really* long time. What if there's something I can't do? Like right now, Dad's just had to help me get my food. What will happen tomorrow, when you're not there? I might starve!'

Mum laughs and puts her arm around my shoulders. 'You will *not* starve, Edie, don't worry about that! It's normal to be a bit worried, and I'm worried too, but I know that you'll be absolutely fine. You are much more capable than you think you are.'

Dad takes a sip of water. 'And you need to remember,

if there's anything you can't do, just ask. I know you, Miss Eckhart – don't be stubborn for the sake of it!'

'Sometimes Dad and I help you a little bit more than you probably need us to,' Mum admits. 'It's only because we love you. But I'm sure you could've got the food here just fine without us!'

'FINISHED!' Louie announces. He's been so busy eating his pizza, he hasn't listened to anything we have been talking about. 'Mummy, please can I have two more slices?'

'I'll get it for you, Lou!' I say, standing up from the table. This is my opportunity to show my parents (and myself), that I can do things on my own.

I walk up to the pizza counter, holding on to the chairs on the way there to keep steady.

'Please can I have two slices of margherita pizza?' I ask the chef behind the counter, getting ready to point at the pizza so that if he doesn't understand *exactly* what I was saying, he knows what I want.

But he seems to understand me perfectly. He places two slices on a plate and hands it to me.

'Thank you,' I say, and I head back to the table, making sure not to drop the pizza on the way back.

I put the plate down in front of Louie.

'YAY, thanks, Didi!' Louie grins and puts the slice of pizza in his mouth. He has no idea how happy I am and how proud I am that I was actually able to go up, talk to a stranger and bring back the food without falling over. He's just happy to be eating his pizza. I don't blame him!

'I did it!' I announce to Mum and Dad, who both grin at me and squeeze my hand.

'Edie Eckhart, you can do anything you set your mind to,' Mum says firmly.

Maybe I'll be OK on this school trip, after all!

Monday 9am

As soon as I woke up this morning, I didn't seem to have any of the worry I had yesterday; all I felt was excitement.

'Now, I've packed some snacks and drinks in your backpack in case you get hungry on the way. But try not to eat them all before you set off!' Mum says. She knows me too well.

It's strange driving to school at half-term. There aren't any cars in the car park, but there is a massive coach at the front of the school.

Mum parks up and grabs my case out of the boot. I can see Flora and Georgia chatting on the pavement, and their mums are behind them talking to each other animatedly.

'Hello!' I yell, and they wave. My friends look as excited as me. Mr Murphy is there too, with a clipboard, ticking off people's names when they arrive.

'Poppy, Tom and Chloe,' he mumbles to himself, ticking them off his list, and I see my three friends walking up towards the coach.

We walk over to where the crowd is gathering.

Mum goes over to Flora's mum. 'You must be Sara! Hello, I'm Angela, Edie's mum.' Mum holds out her hand to shake Sara's, but instead Sara goes in for a hug. Mum looks a bit surprised.

'Sorry, I'm a big hugger!' Sara says. 'And it's so great to finally meet you. We're big Edie fans in our house!'

'Likewise!' Mum responds. 'We all think Flora is marvellous.'

I smile at Flora. She goes bright red, and I can feel myself getting hotter too. I can't explain why, but my mum meeting Flora's mum feels like a big thing. I'm relieved they seem to like each other.

I look around to see if I can spot any other of my friends and I spot a big group of kids I don't know, including a boy, a wheelchair user, with dark hair and glasses. I wave at him and he frowns back at me. I immediately feel silly. I think I only waved at him because I'm disabled too. I wonder who he is.

Mr Murphy sees me looking over at the group.
'That's Bridlington School's drama group,' he explains.
'They're the other school coming on the trip with us.
Ah, here she is. Mrs Hargreaves, Bridlington School's
head of drama.'

A pristine looking woman walks up to Mr Murphy.

I guess she's in her late fifties, and she has grey hair tied up in a bun. She doesn't look like a drama teacher; she looks serious and is wearing a brown skirt with a matching brown jacket. In comparison, Mr Murphy looks like a silly, happy clown.

'Murphy,' she booms. 'Is everybody present and correct?'

Mr Murphy checks his clipboard, 'That's all of my lot here. How about yours?'

Mrs Hargreaves nods. 'They're all getting on the bus now.' She turns to our group. 'Which is where you should be, don't you think?'

Rude! I look over to Mum, who raises her eyebrows, hugs me and whispers in my ear, 'Better do what Miss Trunchbull says or else she'll throw you in the chokey!'

I love the fact that Mum can tell exactly what kind of person somebody is after meeting them for a few seconds. I could already tell that she liked Flora's mum and that she didn't like Mrs Hargreaves. I'd like to think I have a good sense of people too!

Flora and Georgia say bye to their mums too, and we get on the coach. I find a seat near the back of the bus next to Flora.

'Are you excited?' Flora asks, as we drive away from the school and my mum and Sara become small waving dots in the distance.

I nod, but I can't help but feel a bit nervous. I miss Louie already.

To try and distract myself from feeling sad, I unzip my backpack and pull out a packet of crisps.

'Hula Hoop?' I ask Flora, and she takes a few.

I pass them around all of my friends, and soon my nerves and my sadness disappear. I even stop feeling nervous about Mrs (Trunchbull) Hargreaves.

☆☆☆

'We're here!' Mrs Hargreaves announces, waking me up from my nap. I look over at Flora. She has been asleep too, and has been resting her head on my shoulder. At the same time we notice that she has dribbled a bit on my jumper.

She looks embarrassed, and wipes it away. 'Oh no! I'm so sorry.'

'No, I like it,' I joke. 'Now we're both dribblers!'

Flora laughs, and I'm glad I can make her feel less embarrassed about the dribble. I've lost count of the amount of times I've dribbled on her!

I look outside the window of the coach and see nothing but fields and a few cute sheep roaming around. It's so quiet.

'Sir, where is the hotel?' Georgia asks.

Mr Murphy laughs. 'We're camping, Georgia, remember? Hence the sleeping bags.'

'Yeah, but I thought we were just *saying* we were camping. I didn't know we were actually doing it. Won't it be really cold?'

'Complaining already, this bodes well,' Mrs Hargreaves remarks. 'I hope your lot aren't going to moan, Mr Murphy. *Mine* are excellent campers.'

I frown. 'I thought the point of this week was for the two schools to get to know each other,' I whisper to Flora. 'She's already making it into a competition.'

'Something to share with the group?' Mrs Hargreaves asks me, and my tummy drops.

'No, miss.' I look down at the ground because I don't want her to see me going red.

'Right.' Mr Murphy claps his hands. 'First things first, let's pop the tents up!'

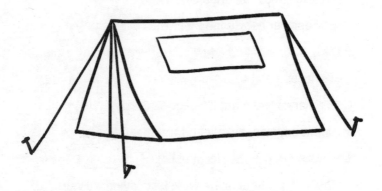

'Pop the tents up' makes it sound easy peasy, but we quickly find that isn't the case. Poppy and Flora take charge and tell me and Georgia what to do. I mainly hold the hooks. Eventually, after what feels like five hours, we get it up. Phew!

☆☆☆

When it gets dark, Mr Murphy lights a fire and we all sit round on logs and sing songs from musicals. When it's my turn to pick what song we should sing, I choose 'Defying Gravity', from the musical *Wicked*. I am not a great singer, but I still give it some welly and I enjoy singing the high, loud parts.

'We definitely have the best tent!' Poppy grins when we go to bed.

I say good night to Poppy, Georgia and Flora and I fall asleep as soon as my head hits the pillow.

Tuesday 6.01am – DAY ONE OF DRAMA CAMP

'Wake up, girls!'

Is it the middle of the night? I am half asleep and I have forgotten where I am.

I force open one eye and slowly, as I begin to wake up, I remember I am in a tent, on the drama trip. My face is the only part of me that is out of the sleeping bag and it is Freezing with a capital F.

'What time is it, miss?' asks Poppy from the sleeping bag next to mine.

'Late! It's six a.m. and the drama bootcamp starts now. You have twenty minutes to shower, get dressed and then I want you to meet me outside in the field for a morning run before breakfast.'

Georgia rolls her eyes. 'How will a morning run help us become better actors?' she whispers.

Mrs Hargreaves scowls. 'A good actor will be fresh, focused and ready for anything. A morning run is the perfect start to the day. Do not question my methods, Georgia Lawson. I hope you're not one of those silly children who only thinks about their hair and makeup!'

Georgia looks down. 'Sorry, miss.'

'Why are half of you still asleep?' Mrs Hargreaves claps her hands and we all jump wide awake. 'Field, twenty minutes!'

Mrs Hargreaves takes her head out of our tent. She is probably going to terrify somebody else's tent.

Flora is somehow already wide awake, and making her way out with a towel draped on her shoulder and her toothbrush in one hand. She sees me struggling a bit to sit up and crawls over to give me a hand out of my sleeping bag.

'Morning, did you sleep well?' she asks, sounding chirpy.

'Yeah, but not for long enough,' I admit, already yawning. 'How come you're so awake when it's the middle of the night?'

Flora laughs. 'It's not the middle of the night! I always wake up at six, to do all my jobs for Mum before I go to school.'

I had no idea Flora did that. 'You get up at six in the morning every single morning? What do you do?'

We make our way out of the tent as Flora lists a whole load of tasks. Washes, cleans, makes lunch for herself, makes her mum's lunch and puts it in the fridge, arranges her mum's pills for the day. Then she wakes her mum up, washes her, dresses her, makes sure she has everything she needs, and when her mum is sorted, Flora gets ready and leaves for school.

Flora doesn't make it sound like this is annoying at all.

'I can't believe you do all that before you even go to school. It's a lot of hard work. Don't you get tired?'

Flora thinks about my question for a second. 'Sometimes. One time I fell asleep in geography because I was so tired. But most of the time I don't really think about it as work. I love my mum and she needs my help, so I just do what needs to be done.'

Wow, Flora is literally a superhero. I can't believe she illustrated me as one last term. She is the definition!

'You two should really hurry up!' Poppy says, brushing her teeth. 'We don't want to get on the wrong side of Mrs Hargreaves.'

'She already hates me,' Georgia says, poking her bottom lip out. 'And now I don't even have anywhere to curl my hair. Why aren't there any plugs in this tent? This is a disaster! I should have stayed behind with Oscar!'

☆☆☆

The morning jog is as cold and wet and as tiring as everybody guessed it would be. The sky is covered in grey clouds and halfway through it starts to rain. The raindrops are so cold on my arms it hurts. Everybody else looks in pain too. Georgia's shivering, and I can see goosebumps on Flora's arms. But nobody complains because we were all terrified of Mrs Hargreaves shouting and making us jog for even longer.

6.45am

'Is she always like this?' I ask a girl from the other school during breakfast. Her name is Lucy and she's very smiley.

She's the only person from the other school who comes to sit with our group. The rest of the other school keep to themselves or stare as if we're from a different planet.

We sit in the middle of the field outside our tents on foldable chairs. Mr Murphy has made us all bacon sandwiches using a little camping stove. It might be because I am starving hungry, but they are seriously delicious. Who knew Mr Murphy would be a good chef!

Lucy nods sadly. 'She's new to our school this year. Drama used to be brilliant, but since she's come, it's got a bit serious. But if we say anything or suggest new ways of doing things, she shouts at us, so it's best for everybody if we just keep our mouths shut and get on with it.'

I think about how much I've loved being part of drama group and how the Christmas play was one of the best things I've ever done. 'I'd hate this week, and Mrs Hargreaves, to ruin drama for me,' I admit to my new friend.

'Just try and ignore her. It's what I do.'

I smile and nod. 'Yeah, I will, thank you.'

But I don't really know how to ignore somebody who seems so mean – and it's only day one!

8.30am

I don't think I've ever been so happy to be indoors. We have walked to the local village hall. It looks like it's about a hundred years old and the paint is peeling off the walls, but I don't care. Anything is better than the field.

Mrs Hargreaves is looking disapproving. 'We don't have time for warm-up games, because you all took too long eating breakfast, so let's crack on with rehearsal, shall we?'

Mrs Hargreaves hands us each a script and tells us that we'll be performing a play called *A Doll's House* by Henrik Ibsen. Typical – another silly play written by a silly man. Why can't we do a play written by a woman? Mrs Hargreaves tells us what it's about, but I don't entirely understand. I think it's basically about a woman who doesn't have a nice husband.

Mrs Hargreaves looks down at the casting list. 'And the person I've decided that will play the lead, Nora, is . . . Flora!' Mrs Hargreaves announces, like she's announcing the winner for *Britain's Got Talent*. She smiles at Flora.

Flora, who wasn't paying attention, looks up at the mention of her name.

'But . . . but . . .' Flora scrambles for words, looking to Mr Murphy for help.

'Flora is our school's set designer, Mrs Hargreaves,' Mr Murphy tries to explain. 'She doesn't act in our shows.'

'Well, perhaps she should take on other roles to get the full experience of dramatic theatre. It will only do her a favour in the long run! Come out of her shell a bit.'

You could see on Mr Murphy's face that this was something he couldn't argue with, but it looked like he was really trying to think of an excuse for Flora.

Just then, Mrs Hargreaves says, 'Mr Murphy, please can you get me a cup of tea?'

Mr Murphy looks a bit shell-shocked, but goes to make her one. Why is she treating him like he's her assistant? He's the best drama teacher in the world!

I see Flora twisting her hands in her lap. She definitely doesn't want the lead role.

'I don't mind playing that Nora woman,' I suggested. 'Maybe I could do that and Flora could do something backstage?'

Flora gave me a squeeze of the arm to thank me for suggesting it, but I think we both knew that once Mrs Hargreaves had decided something, that was that.

Mrs Hargreaves looks at me. 'No, not you, Edie. If you had that role, with the speed of your speech, it would take too long.'

It takes me a few seconds to understand what she means. Is she really saying I can't have a speaking role because I'm *disabled*?

Everybody is looking at me, including my friends. I wish Mr Murphy was here to hear this, but he is still in the kitchen making Mrs Hargreaves a cup of tea. It is clear that nobody knows what to say. So nobody says anything.

☆☆☆

That evening, I get into my sleeping bag. I can't remember a day that's been more tiring.

I had:

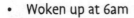

- Woken up at 6am
- Run around a field eight times
- Eaten breakfast and cleared up the dishes afterwards
- Read and rehearsed the play. So far, I am in one scene, and I don't have any lines. I play a maid who comes into the room and puts a pot of tea on the table. It's definitely different from playing Scrooge last term, that's for sure
- Made and eaten dinner (I was in charge of mashing the potatoes – everybody said that was the best bit!)

'Night, Poppy.' I wave to her from the other side of the tent.

'Night, Edie. Hopefully horrible Hargreaves will be a little bit nicer tomorrow!' she whispers, smiling at me.

I hope so too, but I'm not holding my breath.

I turn to face the side of the tent and shut my eyes, which is a relief after the day. Then I feel a tap on my back. I turn back around.

'Hello,' I whisper to Flora, grinning, 'are you OK?'

Flora nods and whispers, 'Can we go outside for a second?' She looks worried. I hope she's all right.

I slither out of my sleeping bag and Flora unzips the tent quietly to make sure we don't wake everybody. Georgia is already quietly snoring away.

'Are you cold?' Flora asks me once we're outside.

'A bit. Let's stand close to each other to keep warm. It's what penguins do. I saw it once in a nature documentary.'

We both huddle together and giggle when our noses touch.

'Thank you for sticking up for me today, even though Hargreaves ignored us. And I'm sorry she was so mean about you. I should have said something but I think my brain was in panic-mode about being given a role. I'm so sorry!'

I shrug. 'Don't worry, I understand. It's only a silly

little play and if I can help you in any way, or help to learn your lines, let me know.'

Flora grabs my hand and kisses it. 'Thank you, Edie. I really, really like you.'

My tummy does somersaults. 'I really, really like you too.'

Flora reaches in her pocket for something, and passes it to me.

'Happy Valentine's Day, Edie.'

I stare at the card. I can't believe Flora has made this for me.

I am just about to open it up when Mrs Hargreaves appears out of nowhere.

'FLORA ITO! EDIE ECKHART! WHAT ARE YOU DOING OUT OF YOUR TENT?'

Mr Hargreaves grabs the card and reads it before I get the chance to. Whatever is written in the card makes Mrs Hargreaves even angrier, because she hisses, 'If I see you two anywhere out here again in the middle of the night, I'll be ringing your mothers and demanding that they come and collect you and take you home. Do I make myself clear?'

I nod and Flora nods. I can tell that Flora is about to cry and I want to ask her if she's OK, but I know that, right now, that would make things worse.

We crawl back into the tent.

When Hargreaves zips up the tent, it is pitch black.

'Are you OK?' Georgia whispers next to me.

'Yes. Night,' I reply as quickly as I can because I don't want to talk about it.

But I am not OK. I am angry that Mrs Hargreaves thinks that it's acceptable to shout at us and I am upset that I never got to read what Flora had written in the card.

I turn away and I cry until I fall asleep. I miss my mum and my dad and Louie and Oscar.

Wednesday 3.19pm – DAY TWO OF DRAMA CAMP

We are only on day two, but it feels like we've been at drama camp for years.

Because Mrs Hargreaves caught me and Flora chatting after lights-out last night, she hasn't let us sit next to each other at all today.

We are rehearsing, but because my role in the play is so small, I'm sitting watching and doing nothing. I am bored. I think about all the things I could be doing if I was at home. I am never leaving my house or my family ever again.

I think back to what Mrs Hargreaves said to me yesterday. I couldn't have a bigger part because I would take too long to read the lines? She was stopping me from doing something because I have cerebral palsy. I wonder if that will happen again to me in my life. I suspect it will, but that doesn't make it right, or fair.

When *will* I feel good enough? Will I ever feel good enough?

I snap back into the room when I hear somebody

mention my name. 'Maybe Edie could do that role. She only has a little part at the moment.'

I smile, because it's so like Poppy to be suggesting ways to involve people, and to do the play differently. I think she's going to be a director when she's older. She's brilliant.

Mrs Hargreaves points her finger at her. 'Poppy! If you don't stop being so bossy, you won't have a role in this production at all!'

Bossy! Poppy isn't bossy. I can't believe it. What kind of teacher is Mrs Hargreaves, anyway? I look around the group and all of my friends. I think she's managed to insult and shout at every single one of them today. She even told Tom to lower his voice. Tom is quite loud, but nobody really cares . . . it's what makes Tom, *Tom*!

Right, I decide. I've had enough. I need to tell Mr Murphy how much of a monster she is. He'll be on my side, I know he will. Where is he anyway?

☆☆☆

I find him on the field doing star jumps. There is nobody

like Mr Murphy! I take a deep breath.

'Mr Murphy, please can I talk to you?'

'Of course, Edie. What's wrong?' Mr Murphy asks, continuing to do star jumps, which if I'm honest is kind of off-putting.

There are so many things I want to say to him, I'm not sure where to start.

'Well, it's er, about Mrs Hargreaves. She's said a few things, and acted in a way which makes me feel, er, not great.'

I trail off slightly. Suddenly I'm unsure whether I should've said anything at all.

'But on this trip Mrs Hargreaves is just as in charge as I am, so what she says goes.' Mr Murphy says, finally stopping jumping to catch his breath.

I give it one more go. 'But, sir, she shouts at everyone. And she favours her class over us lot – they all have better parts apart from Flora. Please, can you tell her to be fair at least?'

Mr Murphy stops jumping and frowns. 'Is this because you haven't been given one of the main roles this time?' he asks me.

'Because you know you can't have the starring part every time we put on a production'.

I swallow. How could Mr Murphy think that this has anything to do with the play, or how big my role is?

I turn to leave, before I say something I can't take back.

☆☆☆

I'm not sure what time it is, but I know it's late. Everybody else is sleeping, and I am writing under my sleeping bag with a torch, trying not to wake the girls up.

I keep thinking about my conversation with Mr Murphy. I really feel like he wasn't listening to me. It's frustrating.

Whenever I think about home, I feel sad. I can't believe I had to persuade my parents to let me come on the trip. If I'd known it was going to be like this, I wouldn't have bothered. I could be at home right now, in my warm bed, waiting for Louie to come in for a morning cuddle.

I suddenly feel like I want to write something about
Mum and Dad and Louie. I scribble down a poem.

I love my mum, Angela,
I love her loud laugh and her massive smile,
I love how she burns every meal,
And I love her sense of style.

I love my dad, Steve,
I love his hugs and his silly jokes,
I love how he looks after children at work,
And I love when he lets us drink Cokes!

I love my brother, Louie,
I love his appetite and his floppy hair,
I love how he calls me 'Didi',
And I love his amazed, wide-eyed stare!

I read the poem back and I smile. Three more sleeps until
I can see my three favourite people in the world.
I can't WAIT.

I get my phone out.

I have a text from my mum.

> Hiya mushroom. Hope you're having fun on the trip. I can't WAIT to see you on stage at drama camp. So proud of you. Love you so much xxx

I read it and I immediately want to cry. I think about hugging Mum. It feels so long since I saw her.

> Hi Mum. I really don't like it here. I miss you. Please could you come and pick me up now?

I read it back and think about it again. Does it feel a bit drastic to suddenly leave?

I feel guilty about lying to Mum but I really don't want her to worry about me. I re-write the message:

> Hi Mum, I'm having such a great time! See you in a few days xxx

I press send.

Thursday 8.02pm – DAY THREE OF DRAMA CAMP

I haven't written in my diary today because there hasn't been a lot to say, and Mrs Hargreaves has been as mean as ever.

We spent most of the day rehearsing the silly play. Flora tries hard, but everybody can see that she isn't enjoying it. At one point I thought that Flora was going to burst out crying, but she managed to carry on, even when Mrs Hargreaves told her that she was doing it all wrong.

As a midweek treat, Mr Murphy convinced Mrs Hargreaves to let us order pizza, and we all sat in a circle outside by the fire. I ate so much of the Hawaiian one, because most people think it is gross to have pineapple on a pizza, but I think it's de-li-cious!

It was my job to tidy the boxes away after dinner, so I stacked them up until the pile was nearly as tall as me.

'Right, bed,' Mrs Hargreaves commands.

I look at my watch. It's barely eight. I'm allowed to stay up until nine at home, even on a school night! For the millionth time that week I wonder why Mrs Hargreaves is such a meanie.

'Oh bed already, Mrs Hargreaves? But it's such a clear night. I thought we might take a walk in the woods,' Mr Murphy suggests. Is he finally standing up to her? This might be a break through!

Mrs Hargreaves looks at him as if he's just said the most bizarre thing in the world, like he's just suggested that we spend the night sleeping on our heads! 'Don't you think the actors ought to head to bed? They need to be fresh and focused for rehearsals tomorrow.' It's less of a question and more of a demand.

Mr Murphy shrugs. 'Twenty minutes won't do anybody any harm. How about it?'

'Well, Mr Murphy, you can do whatever you want with your group, but my lot are going straight to their tents.'

There was sea of groans from the other school. Lucy, the girl I spoke to on the first day, groaned the loudest.

'Miss, if they get to go for a night walk, why can't we?' she pleaded.

'Because I am in charge of you and that is that!'

I look around at the girls and Tom. We try desperately to hide our smiles from the other group. It wouldn't be nice to rub it in their faces.

Instead, we collect our torches and follow Mr Murphy across the field and into the woods. He asks that we walk in pairs, and without even speaking Flora squeezes my arm and I link mine through hers. I feel so happy that she is my partner. With her next to me I'll be less frightened of all the creepy crawlies.

'This is seriously cool,' Tom grins, striding next to Mr Murphy as we get to the wood. 'Thanks, sir.'

'Well, I thought we couldn't go camping without a little exploring, could we? Now, stick to your pairs, and don't go far enough that I can't see you. But apart from that, please, go forth and explore.'

This is exciting. The ground is wet and slippery, so I cling on to Flora extra tightly.

'Are you OK?' she asks me.

'Yes, but you do know that if I go down, you're coming down with me!' I joke, and Flora laughs.

'Are *you* OK?' I ask her, and we both know that I am asking her generally, about the week.

Flora hesitates, and then speaks so quietly I have to lean in to hear what she is saying.

'I don't know what I'm doing here, Edie. I'm not an actor, I'm rubbish at it. Mrs Hargreaves doesn't understand. I'm a designer, not a performer.'

'But sometimes it's good to be out of your comfort zone – it makes you discover things you never knew about yourself,' I suggest.

'So far the only thing I've discovered this week is that I am seriously bad at learning lines.'

I think back to Christmas, when I played Scrooge in the play. Dad stayed up late with me learning the lines.

'Well maybe, before we go to bed, I'll help you go over them. That way, you'll go to sleep thinking about the lines, and by tomorrow you will know them all, easy peasy!'

'Thanks, Edie. That would be great.' Flora looks at me and smiles, already relaxing her shoulders. I'm pleased that I could make her feel slightly better about the play.

I hesitate. Because she's been so honest with me, I want to be honest with her.

'At least you know who you are,' I say in a small voice. 'I've got no idea who I am.'

Flora furrows her eyebrows in confusion. 'What do you mean?'

I take a deep breath. 'I got a detention last week because I didn't actually complete the English homework where we had to talk about who we are. Because I don't know who I am. I don't know if I know anything at all any more.'

Flora reaches for my hand and squeezes it. 'You don't need to have all of the answers, all of the time, Edie Eckhart! I know you like to have everything sorted, but we're not adults. And even when we *are* adults, we still won't have all of the answers, and that is OK!'

I laugh.

'My mum is an adult,' Flora continues. 'And until last week she thought penguins lived in igloos!'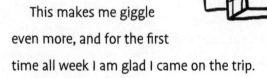

This makes me giggle even more, and for the first time all week I am glad I came on the trip.

'Right, exploration over.' Mr Murphy claps. 'Bed is calling.'

We head out of the wood and to our tents. I hold Flora's arm tightly, and not because I am scared of falling over any more, but because I want to be close to her.

Friday 11.36am – FINAL DAY OF DRAMA CAMP

'OK, now we're going to play a drama game.' Mrs Hargreaves tells us.

Finally! I can't believe we've been here for four days and we haven't played any games. All we've done is rehearse the stupid play, which is way too moody and serious for us. The only thing that has changed for the better is that waking up at six feels normal.

But seriously, this play . . . Even the older students seem annoyed, and Mrs Hargreaves probably shouts at them even more than she shouts at us lot.

'For this, you'll be in pairs.'

I immediately look around the room for Flora. I know that she gets a bit shy if she has to play a game in front of people, or talk to people she doesn't know. If I go with her, I can talk for us both *and* it'll be a good excuse to hang out. I haven't spoken to her properly in front of Mrs Hargreaves since the card incident; I think we've both been worried that we'll get told off again.

I find Flora sitting at the other side of the room and

we grin at each other as if we're silently saying, 'Yes! Let's be each other's partners for the game!'. *This should be fun,* I think.

Mrs Hargreaves's voice shatters the moment. 'Don't be thinking that this is an opportunity to have fun with your friends though. *I* will be placing you in pairs.'

Oh no! I won't get to be with Flora? Hopefully I'll be put with somebody I know at least. I look around for Georgia, Poppy or Chloe.

'Edie, you can go with Myles.'

Who is Myles? He must be somebody from the other school. Probably someone who has been ignoring our school all week!

I see the wheelchair user, the boy who I waved at before we got on the coach on Monday, coming towards me.

I haven't spoken to him all week, because he just talks to his friends, plus I still feel a bit silly for waving at him for no reason.

This might not be so bad, I guess. It could be a good opportunity to speak to someone new. And I haven't got a friend who is also disabled. This could be my chance.

'Hello, I'm Edie.' I smile, and I hold out my hand. It feels a bit formal, but Myles doesn't look like a hugging person, so I think it's the better option.

He looks at my hand as if it's the most disgusting thing he's ever seen and turns to Mrs Hargreaves to wait for the instructions. I take my hand away and feel foolish.

Mrs Hargreaves explains the game to us. 'For this task, I want you to all get to know your partner. You need to trust them.'

We listen as Mrs Hargreaves tells us she will blindfold one of us, while the other person guides us around the room, and eventually outside, around a few obstacles in the field. It sounds like it'll be a lot of fun!

'Do you want to be the one who gets blindfolded, or shall I?' I ask Myles.

'We can't play this game,' Myles says, taking out his phone from his pocket.

He calls Mrs Hargreaves over. 'Mrs Hargreaves,' he says. 'We won't be playing this game. I can't do it, and obviously Emily can't do it either.'

I look around the room to see who 'Emily' is before

realising that he means me, and he's just got my name wrong. I find myself flushing and wait for Mrs Hargreaves to set him straight, and tell him that I'm actually called Edie.

'Of course, Myles, you two can stay here if you like. We'll start rehearsal in twenty minutes.'

So now I'm not able to play the one fun game of the week? I am too surprised to be angry.

'Why did you tell her that we couldn't take part in the game?' I ask as Mrs Hargreaves stalks off. 'I'm sure we could've given it a good go!'

Myles glances up from his phone and looks at me without saying anything, a bit like he feels sorry for me, but I don't know why.

'With me in this chair and you walking like that, we'd be a disaster, and we wouldn't win anyway – so what's the point?'

I didn't think it was about winning and I don't like how he said, 'with you walking like that'. But we've got to be together until the game is over, so I take a deep breath. Maybe he just doesn't like playing physical games. I decide to give him the benefit of the doubt.

'Well, shall we have a chat instead then?' I suggest. 'And just so you know, my name is Edie, not Emily.'

'Whatever,' Myles says, under his breath.

He clearly has no interest in chatting, so I look around the hall. I catch eyes with Mr Murphy, who immediately strides up to me, looking concerned.

'Is everything OK, Edie?'

I look over at Myles, who is still on his phone. 'I don't think I have a partner, sir.'

He glances at Myles, and raises his eyebrows slightly. 'Of course you have a partner . . . me!'

Mr Murphy puts the blindfold on and I have to stop myself from laughing. He looks really funny.

It takes me ages to instruct him around the obstacles,

but that doesn't matter. We both have such a fun time, and when we eventually finish, everybody cheers and claps. I am so pleased I did it!

Friday 5pm – THE PERFORMANCE

It's finally time for the performance of A Doll's House.
All our parents and guardians have come to watch
us. They all look very excited to watch the play . . .
especially because they haven't seen us in five
whole days!

I peep round the door and I see that my parents and
Louie are sitting with Flora and Georgia's mums. It's
great to see them. I'm tempted to run over and give
them a huge hug, but I decide to wait.

I should have the same excited feeling I had before
we performed A Christmas Carol at school, but for some
reason it feels completely different.

'Edie, I don't think I can do this.' It's Flora, who is
wearing her costume. She looks so pale, I think that she's
about to be sick.

I give her an encouraging smile. 'You can, it's only a
few scenes, and after it's over, you don't have to perform
on stage ever again.' I kiss her cheek. 'Good luck. I'll be
here the whole time.'

'This is what we've all been working towards this

week at bootcamp,' Mrs Hargreaves booms. 'Do not embarrass me.'

'Yeh, great pep talk,' Georgia sighs under her breath as she looks in the mirror. Her hair is really big, and I think it looks lovely but I can tell that she hates it. Every morning she's tried to curl her hair, and every morning Mrs Hargreaves stops her from doing it, claiming that there's 'no time for grooming'.

We enter the village hall via the back. There's no stage, so we have to perform on the same level as the audience. Poor Flora has to walk all the way to the front in her enormous dress with everyone looking at her.

The play starts. I am one of the first people on. I pat down my costume – a maid's uniform with a little white hat – and get ready to go on the 'stage'.

As I walk on, Mum waves at me from her seat in the back. I don't say anything in this bit, just open the door to Flora, playing Nora, then go back off.

Every time Flora has lines, I stand up on my tiptoes and watch her from off stage. Flora forgets a few of her lines but considering we only started rehearsing the play four days ago, she does really well. I'm proud of her!

Then it's my turn again. I go on, announce the visitors and leave again. It goes so quickly, I barely remember it.

When I'm performing, I look at my parents in the audience. They beam at me, but in between them is a sleeping Louie. I don't blame him! It's a boring play, so if I could, I would be sleeping through it too!

I look over at the back of the hall and see Mr Murphy. He gives me two thumbs up. At least he's happy.

☆☆☆

'Ooh, and the way you introduced the house guests on stage was magnificent. What a professional,' my mum chirps.

We're driving back home, at long last.

'Yes, that's our girl!' my dad agrees. 'Have you enjoyed being away, love?'

I hesitate.

'I liked spending time with my friends and cooking and cleaning, but I missed you three, so I'm glad to be coming home.'

'You liked cleaning, eh?' my dad asks me, raising an

eyebrow. 'Well, you can do more of that as soon as we get home!'

I laugh and roll my eyes. But if I'm honest, I wouldn't mind cleaning at all; I'm just happy to be away from that monster Hargreaves and back with my amazing family!

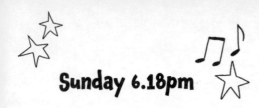

Sunday 6.18pm

I read out the poem I wrote at camp after tea. Mum, Dad
and Louie clap enthusiastically.

'We love Edie the poet!' Mum grabs my face and
kisses my cheek, 'but do I really burn *every* meal?'

Without talking, all four of us look down at the
remains of the lasagne on our plates. The dish is burnt at
the corners and half the garlic bread has been left
because it is so black.

'OK,' my mum puts her hands up as if she's being
arrested, 'point taken.'

'Well, I LOVED it!' my dad announces, pouring all of
the remaining lasagne on to his plate and tucking into it.
'More for me!'

We all laugh so much it hurts!

Thursday 1.28pm

The bell rings for the end of lunchtime.

We're sitting on our usual bench. All week, we've been telling Oscar and Pip how properly rubbish the trip was.

'I'm not bossy, am I bossy?' Poppy keeps asking us. We all say no. It's not quite the truth – I suppose some people might think Poppy was bossy. But she's also amazing at being in charge and kind and thoughtful, so it's a good thing. It's why we all love Poppy so much!

Georgia is much happier now that she has time to curl her hair, but Flora shivers every time we mention the play.

'But did you enjoy performing, Flora, when you were actually up there on stage?' Oscar asks now.

'No! Definitely not! I hated every minute!'

'You were really good though, Flora,' Tom says, smiling.

The bell rings and we head to our classes. I have English, so me and Pip walk over together.

'See you tonight at drama club,' Georgia yells to me as she heads up the corridor to maths.

'Ah, I can't go tonight, we have too much English homework,' I say. 'See you tomorrow.'

I turn back around, link my arm through Pip's and we make our way to class.

'We don't have any English homework, Edie.' Pip says with a concerned look on her face, as soon as she knows Georgia can't hear us.

I shrug. 'I just don't feel like going to the group tonight.'

Friday 4.28pm

Dad comes into the living room where I'm sitting on the sofa about to watch TV.

'Right,' he says grinning and perching on the arm of the sofa, 'your mum's out with her friends, Louie's at Ralph's. It's time for you to be initiated.'

I am super confused. I've just got home from school. What on earth does he mean?

Dad laughs at my serious expression. 'Change out of your school uniform and meet me at the door in ten minutes, OK?'

I walk upstairs and my phone beeps. It's Oscar.

Do you fancy coming round to
my house tonight to watch films?

Sorry I can't, I'm going somewhere with my dad,
but he's being very weird and secretive about it.

OSCAR

LOL, have fun, see you at the weekend!
Keep me posted with what you're doing.

I meet my dad downstairs.

'Where are we going, Dad? Why are you being secretive?'

He offers me his arm and we leave the house and start walking down the road.

'We're going to the pub, Edie Eckhart!'

'But Dad, I'm only twelve!'

Dad shakes his head. 'I know that, Edie! But you're my little girl so it's about time for you to properly appreciate a good pub. Don't worry, you'll be on the lemonade!'

☆☆☆

The pub is quiet – practically empty. At the bar, my dad orders a pint, and a lemonade for me.

He comes back to our table. 'Here we go, missus. Welcome to the Real Ale Club!'

'Who else is in the club?' I ask him, taking the glass.

'Nobody!' my dad giggles. 'It's just me.'

'Do you come here a lot, Dad? And do you drink a lot of beer?' I ask him, feeling a bit worried. I don't know if I like the idea of him drinking on his own.

My dad takes a sip of his beer and swallows slowly. He shakes his head. 'Not at all. Most of the time I only drink one pint of beer. Sometimes two, but it's not about drinking, it's about having a place that you can come every now and then and have a little think on your own. That's just for me!'

This all makes sense now, and I love my dad for showing me his special spot.

I think about everything I've done over the past few months. It's (mostly) been brilliant, but I've spent every single day with either my friends or family. It's tiring. Maybe my dad is suggesting I need some time on my own, just to think about stuff. I think he might be right.

'Thank you for letting me into your little secret, Dad.'

We lift our drinks up and clink them together. 'Cheers!'

Later in the night, when my dad goes to the loo, I message Oscar.

> **We're at the pub!!!** 🍺 😆

OSCAR

For the rest of the evening, me and Dad chat a little bit
– about school, and work, and stuff like that – but
mostly we sit there in silence, and it's really nice not
feeling like I have to talk.

It's exactly what I need.

Saturday 10.36am

'Mum,' I plead, 'do I really need to go food shopping with you? Can't I stay here and finish reading my book?'

I usually enjoy going shopping, but today it's cold and rainy and I just want to stay inside under a blanket and keep dry and warm.

'No you can't, you lazy sausage. Come on, Louie's already got his shoes and coat on!'

'I'm Mummy's favourite!' Louie giggles, and I know he's probably right.

☆☆☆

We're in the cereal aisle, but it's taking for ever because Louie keeps picking one and then changing his mind.

'Edie, I forgot the strawberry yoghurt back there, please can you go to the dairy aisle and pick me some up?' Mum says.

I reluctantly agree and make my way back to the fridges.

'Edie!' I hear somebody say as I walk down the aisle. I look up and I can't believe who it is.

'Mrs Adler!'

She's pushing a big trolley, with two baby seats at the front.

'Hello, girls, this is Edie,' she says, turning the trolley round to face me. 'Edie was a pupil in my class before you two monkeys got in the way.' Mrs Adler leans closer to the babies and whispers loudly, 'She was my favourite student!'

I smile. The girls are both so cute. They are dressed exactly the same, in matching green dungarees with dinosaurs on. There is only one difference: one has a yellow bow in her hair, and one has a purple bow.

'What are their names?' I ask Mrs Adler.

'This is Anya,' she says, pointing at the frowning baby with the yellow bow, 'and this is Lily,' pointing at the nearly asleep baby with the purple bow.

'How do you know which one is which?' I ask her.

'Well, Anya is a grumpy guts, and Lily will sleep absolutely anywhere. Look! She's nearly asleep now!'

It's true; in the middle of the supermarket Lily has

just shut her eyes and fallen straight to sleep.

I touch Anya's cheek, and I tickle her feet gently. 'Hello, Anya, my name is Edie.'

Suddenly, Anya stops frowning and smiles.

'Ohhhh what an honour! She likes you, Edie. She doesn't usually smile for anybody.'

I grin at Mrs Adler and look back at the babies.

'Babe, what's the name of the granola you like again?' A lady walks up to us holding a big box of cereal. She has really short blonde hair, a denim jacket and super cool boots which have loads of little studs on the side. She looks like she would ride a motorbike.

'Beth, this is Edie, you know—'

The woman interrupts Mrs Adler. 'From your tutor group! Oh hello, Edie. This one talks about you a lot!'

I'm glad that Mrs Adler hasn't forgotten me completely.

Mum comes round the corner holding Louie's hand. 'Edie! How long does it take to get a few yoghurts— oh, hello there.'

'Mum, this is Mrs Adler, you know, my tutor who went off to have babies, and this is her wife, and these are the babies, Lily and Anya!'

Mum loves babies as much as I do and immediately leans down to say hello to them. Lily is still asleep, and Anya just frowns at her.

'Edie got a little smile out of our frowner,' Mrs Adler says, beaming at me.

'Oh they're both so adorable,' my mum coos. 'It makes me want to have another one – or two!'

I would love that. I remember when Louie was a baby like it was yesterday. Even though I was only seven, I remember holding him and hugging him and never wanting to let him go!

'Edie, I want to catch up with you properly,' Mrs Adler says. She turns to my mum. 'How long do you plan on shopping for? Maybe Edie and I could go for a quick drink in the café, what do you think?'

'Of course, I take for ever in here, which annoys Edie. I'm sure she'll be keen to get away!'

Beth smiles. 'And I'm sorry, babe, but I can do the shopping much quicker if you're not here perusing down each and every aisle!'

Mrs Adler turns to me and asks, 'Well then, if I'm not

needed here, do you fancy a little drink and a natter?'

There's nothing I want to do more!

I sit down at a table at the supermarket café while Mrs
Adler orders. I watch her talking to the person behind the
counter. It's weird to see her out of school, wearing
normal clothes. She's wearing light blue jeans, black
boots and a floral shirt. She looks very pretty. Her hair,
which somehow looks redder and curlier than I
remember, bounces on her shoulders as she walks up to
me, smiling.

She puts the hot chocolate down in front of me.

'I've got cake too! Chocolate or carrot?'

What a dilemma! I love chocolate AND carrot cake.
This is a hard decision.

'Or we could have half each?' she suggests, sitting
down and taking a sip of her coffee.

'What a brilliant idea, Mrs Adler!'

She smiles as she cuts the cakes in half, and passes
me a plate.

'So how have you been? It feels like ages since I saw you. You look older!' Mrs Adler says. 'Are you taller?'

I shake my head. 'I don't think so, miss. I'm still the shortest person in the class! But I did have a birthday, I'm twelve now.' I think about all the things I've done since my birthday in December. I want to tell Mrs Adler everything, including the drama trip, but I think it would take about eighty-two hours!

I start by telling her the thing that I've wanted to say since it happened. Because she's the only person who I think would understand. I can't hold it in any longer.

'I kissed my friend after the play last term. Her name is Flora and I really like her,' I say.

Mrs Adler looks thoughtful.

Maybe I shouldn't have said anything, I think. Even though we're not at school now, she's still a teacher.

'Sorry,' I say. 'I don't know why I told you, I just wanted to talk to somebody who's, erm . . . people have asked me if I'm gay, and I don't know what to say. How do you know? How did *you* know? I don't even know if I want to be *anybody's* girlfriend. Also we did this assignment about who we are at school, and I decided I don't know, like, how am I supposed to know who I am, never mind who I want to be. I feel like everybody around me has all of the answers and everything and I'm here not knowing anything. I can't even decide what cake I want!'

I feel like I have been talking for a long time, so to shut myself up for a bit I shove a big bit of carrot cake in my mouth.

'This is really good carrot cake.' I grin at Mrs Adler, trying to change the subject.

Mrs Adler takes another sip of her coffee. 'I'm so glad you feel as if you can talk to me. That was just a lot of things to process in a short amount of time.' She smiles, and places her hand gently on my arm. 'But I think the thing you need to remember above all else is that it's OK not to have all of the answers. It's even OK not to have *any* of the answers.'

I sigh. 'Flora said that too, but I want to be like a grown-up, and have it all sorted out. I *really* want to know who I am.'

'But Edie, I'm a thirty-five-year-old woman and I don't *really* know who I am. Everybody changes and adapts. It's perfectly normal to be different things to different people. If you knew everything at your age, the rest of your life would be boring. At twelve-years-old I thought I wanted to be a soap star in Australia. But looking back now, I think I just really fancied Kylie Minogue.'

I smile, already feeling lighter for talking to Mrs Adler. I feel like can trust her.

'It's OK not to know if you want to call yourself gay,' she goes on. 'It's OK to never know, or to change your mind. All that matters is that you like who you are, and you stay true to yourself. And about Flora – as long as you like hanging out with Flora, it really doesn't matter what you describe yourself as. Edie Eckhart, you're a thinker, and that's why you and I get on so well. But maybe we both sometimes think *too* much! What I would say is, Flora sounds great and smart and if you enjoy spending time with her, you should keep on doing so.'

I smile and nod in total agreement. She is exactly right. I think A LOT, to a point where sometimes I completely overthink, instead of going with what I feel.

I finish my half of the chocolate cake at the same

time as Mum, Louie, Beth, the babies and two massive trolleys full of bags come round the corner.

'Beth, I leave you for twenty minutes and you've bought the entire shop!' Mrs Adler jokes.

Beth shrugs. 'Never let me loose in a supermarket when I'm hungry.'

'Right, love, are you ready to go?' Mum asks me, and I nod, batting off the cake crumbs on my legs as I stand up.

I hug Mrs Adler goodbye. As we walk away, I can't help but already miss her a little bit.

As if she can read my mind, she shouts after me, 'Don't worry, I'll be back in the summer term – someone has to make sure you stay out of trouble!'

I turn back and grin, then push the trolley out of the supermarket with Mum and Louie.

'It looks like you two were having a good chat,' Mum says. 'Sometimes it's helpful to have a grown-up to talk to who isn't a parent.'

'Yeah,' I say. And she's exactly right.

Sunday 4.54pm

'Edie, stop dribbling!' Dad calls. He's surprised because I don't dribble much any more. I used to dribble all of the time because of my cerebral palsy. When I first started school, Mum had to pack extra sweatshirts because the first would be soaking wet by break time.

Over time, I have got better at swallowing. I think people who aren't disabled swallow automatically, but even now I have a little voice in my head that has to say, 'Swallow, Edie' every few seconds.

Now I just dribble if I'm super tired – or hungry.

'This isn't a disability thing, Dad,' I tell him. 'It's a hungry thing. I keep looking at the gravy. If I had my way, I'd just slurp down the entire jug. I love gravy so much.'

'I know you do, love, but hands off.' Mum taps my hand playfully with a floppy spatula. 'We need to wait for Grandad Eric before we start tucking in.'

I look at the clock and it's nearly five. That's weird. Grandad Eric always comes at half four if he comes round for Sunday dinner and he is never late.

At that moment, the front door opens.

'Call off the search party, I'm here.' Grandad Eric walks into the kitchen. He is wearing a big raincoat and woolly hat. He looks a bit different, but I can't work out why.

'Are you OK, Dad?' Mum walks towards him. 'Not like you to be late.'

Grandad Eric takes his hat off, then his coat. 'I'm fine. Had a funny turn, but I'm right as rain now.'

'Eric, what do you mean by "a funny turn"?' Dad asks him, in a voice that I like to call his 'serious doctor voice'.

Grandad Eric pretends to bat both my mum and dad away with his hand and sits down at the table. 'Just felt a bit dizzy. Stop fussing you two and let me eat my bodyweight in roast potatoes.'

He grins at me and whispers, 'I'm surprised you haven't drunk all of the gravy already!'

'I would have, if Mum hadn't stopped me.'

'Spoil sports,' he says and winks at me.

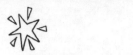

Wednesday 3.45pm

I'm waiting for Oscar to finish his art class. Art is one of his favourite subjects this year – he really likes his teacher, Miss Jamison. She's tall and she is quite posh. I think she's from London. She always wears brilliantly bright clothes. I've decided I would like to dress like her when I'm older.

'Come on, Oscar,' I say under my breath. I hate waiting around school longer than I need to. We could be home already watching a film or playing a game but instead I'm here, waiting, like a lemon.

'Edie, are you lurking in the corridor?'

I jump – I had no idea that there was anybody else here. I look up and see Mr Murphy.

'No, sir. I am waiting for my friend Oscar.'

Mr Murphy frowns. 'I haven't seen you in drama club recently, Edie. The group are starting to miss you.'

I look at the floor because I don't know what to say. 'I've just had a lot of homework on recently. I'll try and come tomorrow.'

'I hope so, Edie. It would be a shame if you stopped

coming completely. As I said before, you are very talented.'

I give a little nod. I look at the floor until Mr Murphy walks away.

Friday 3.05pm

I look at the clock and stare at the second hand. I am convinced that time moves slower on a Friday afternoon. It's almost as if the clock knows that it's nearly the weekend, so it decides to torture us!

What makes it even worse is that my last lesson on a Friday is geography, which I find incredibly boring. I just don't care about rocks and stuff.

There's a knock on the door and Mrs Everett comes in. She's been at the school for ever; she even taught my mum when she came to the school. I don't see much of her, but she's the deputy head teacher and everybody's pretty scared of her.

'I'd like to have a word with Edie Eckhart,' she says. Then she turns to me and says, 'Bring your bag with you, Edie.'

But why? Am I in trouble?? I haven't missed any of my homework for a while. I suppose sometimes I am late for class, but not all the time.

Everyone looks at me as I slowly stand up from my table, collect my stuff and walk to the front of the classroom. My brain is thinking at a million miles an hour, trying to work out why Mrs Everett wants to talk to me.

We walk down the corridor in silence until we reach her office. We go in and Mrs Everett shuts the door behind us.

Oscar is there wearing his backpack. Which makes it even more confusing.

'Are you all right, Osc?' I ask him, and he nods, but doesn't say anything, which is odd. He doesn't look OK. 'What's going on?'

Mrs Everett says, 'Edie, your grandad has been taken unwell and been admitted to hospital. They're going to keep him in for a few days. He has severe stomach pains, and they are just going to do a few tests on him. Your mum is with him, and your dad is working, so if it's OK with you, you're going to go back with Oscar after school. Your mum says not to worry about Louie – he's at a friend's house. She'll call you later.'

My eyes sting. This can't be happening. Grandad Eric

was fine yesterday. He was just a bit dizzy!

'You and Oscar can leave school early, and I'll check in with you on Monday. Try not to worry, Edie – he's in good hands. I'll be thinking of you.'

She opens her office door and Oscar and I leave. I can tell that he doesn't really know what to say.

'Do you like chicken?' he asks at last, quietly, and I know what this means. I link my arm through his, taking a wing.

Saturday 10.30am

I slept over at Oscars. My mum rang me last night and told me about Grandad Eric. He fainted when he was walking to the shops, and now the doctors think there's something wrong with his stomach, so they're keeping him in the hospital for more tests. Mum seemed OK when she rang me, but I could tell that she'd been crying.

Mum said Louie is staying with Ralph, and she's decided not to tell him about Grandad Eric for the time being. I think that's the right decision, because it would only make him upset.

'Do you want to go bowling?' Oscar asks me.

I shake my head.

'Do you want to go to the cinema?' he suggests.

Again, I don't say anything at all, I just shake my head.

'What do you want to do then?'

I shrug. 'Oscar, do you mind if I sit here on the sofa on my own for a bit?'

'Er, yeah, OK then.'

Oscar leaves the living room and I can tell that he

doesn't really know what to do. I always do all of the talking, but right now I don't feel like it.

I just want to be on my own and think about my Grandad Eric.

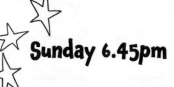

Sunday 6.45pm

'I picked out the balloon for you, Grandad Eric!' Louie sings, jumping to sit on his hospital bed.

'Careful, Lou, he's just had an operation,' Dad warns him.

I sit next to the bed. Grandad Eric looks pale and he has a lot of tubes going from his nose and his arm into lots of different machines making beeping sounds. It's all a bit confusing.

'Blue is my favourite colour, Louie lad,' Grandad Eric says, trying to sound as cheery as possible, but I can tell he is in a lot of pain.

'I thought it was! I told Daddy that I think your favourite colour is blue and it is!'

I hold Grandad Eric's hand and he tries to squeeze it back, but it is only a weak squeeze.

'How long do you think you'll be in here, Grandad?' I ask him.

'Hopefully the day after tomorrow, Edie love, if my bloods stay level, whatever that means.'

'Good. And then you can stay with us. Where I can watch you and stop you from eating any silly chillies,' my mum says, sounding more worried than angry.

The doctors told us that Grandad Eric had fainted because he had lost blood due to an ulcer in his stomach. Ulcers sometimes happen when you eat too much hot food. And Grandad Eric *loves* hot sauce. He puts it on every food you can imagine . . . even on his roast dinner!

'Would you believe it?' Grandad Eric chuckles. 'Almost killed by a chilli! What a way to go!'

I can't help but laugh too, feeling relieved that Grandad Eric will be OK.

Tuesday 7.58pm

I sit on Grandad Eric's bed. He's staying in the spare bedroom at the front of the house. It's usually the room that everybody uses to store random rubbish when we don't know what to do with it, but now it is Grandad's temporary place to stay.

'I don't know, Grandad Eric! Mum told me that I needed to let you get your rest, and it's getting late.'

Grandad Eric waves his hand, like he always does when somebody says something he doesn't agree with. 'Ohhh but I'm feeling right as rain again! Go on, play one more song from your Spotatune.'

I laugh, knowing that he means Spotify. I pick a song that I know he loves: *My Girl* by The Temptations.

'Oh this is one of my favourite songs,' he says as soon as it comes on, and he starts singing along. He's croakier than normal, and keeps shutting his eyes, as if he's the sleepiest person in the entire world.

I join in with the singing, using a television remote

control as a pretend microphone. Grandad Eric laughs at me. 'Whenever you perform, Edie, your whole blooming face lights up. I love watching you.'

'This isn't performing, Grandad!' I tell him. 'This is just me having a bit of fun with you.'

'But isn't that what life is, love?' he asks. 'Isn't it all about just having a bit of fun? When I saw you at Christmas, playing that Scrooge, I've never seen you look so happy. You were brilliant, and I'm not even biased! Your mum said you were brilliant playing a maid in the drama-camp play. When is your next performance?'

I shrug. 'I've kind of stopped going to drama club.'

Grandad Eric frowns. 'Why is that, love?'

I sit down next to Grandad Eric's bed in the armchair. 'I don't feel like a performer any more,' I admit. 'There was this teacher at the drama camp and she didn't make me feel good about performing. I don't know, maybe I'm not meant to be an actor. Maybe I should stick to writing.'

I was talking to Grandad Eric, but the more I spoke, the more it felt like I was speaking to myself. It felt so good to say the things I've just been thinking in my head for the past few weeks out loud.

'Well, let me tell you, if I ever meet this so-called teacher, I'll give them a piece of my mind!' Grandad Eric waves his finger in anger. 'Edie, you don't need to know everything right now. You don't have to know exactly what you want to do when you're older. All you need to do now is have fun. And if drama feels fun, then you should go for it. Do you hear me?'

I smile at him. For a sick guy, he still speaks a lot of sense.

'Don't ever listen to anybody but yourself, Edie. Promise me? You know yourself better than anyone else.'

I think he might be right.

Thursday 3.25pm

I walk into the hallway for drama, feeling a bit nervous. What if Mr Murphy is annoyed that I've missed so many classes? What if he throws me out before class begins?

Everybody is already in the hall, sitting in a circle. I quickly put my bag down at the side and find a spot in between Georgia and Poppy.

'Yay! You're back!' Poppy whispers. Georgia gives me a squeeze.

I look over to the stage to see Flora in her painting overalls, already with paint on her cheek. She waves at me.

'Nice for you to grace us all with your presence, Eckhart.' Mr Murphy grumbles, but I can tell he's happy to see me.

I feel excited. Like I'm going to enjoy this. In a way that disappeared during the drama trip. That week wasn't about what drama really is.

But here with my group, ready to play and have fun and test myself – this is what I love.

Friday 9.04pm

Sleepover time! We're at Georgia's house, and we have taken over her living room with a million blankets and pillows. It is *so cosy*!

'Please don't make us watch another scary movie again, Chloe!' Poppy pleads.

'Last time we watched one, Edie jumped so high she spilled all of the popcorn,' Georgia giggled.

It was true. Last year, Chloe made us watch a film about a haunted house and a girl who lives in the cellar, and I got so frightened, I threw the bowl of popcorn right up in the air, and it covered all four of us – me, Chloe, Poppy and Georgia. At breakfast the next day, Poppy found a piece of popcorn in her hair, which must've been there all night!

'But that's the point of scary stuff! It's the jumping, it's never knowing what's around the corner,' Chloe says in her scariest voice.

Someone appears from round the corner and we all jump, including Chloe! 'Only me,' Georgia's mum says.

175

'Oops, sorry for making you jump. I've brought you some more snacks.'

Georgia's mum is the queen of snacks – she has an entire drawer in her kitchen dedicated to them. Crisps, nuts, chocolate, sweets – you name it, she has it. When I'm older I've already decided I want a snack drawer.

'Thank you, Mrs Lawson!' we all shout. She pops the crisps and the nuts down and leaves.

Georgia grabs a handful of Twiglets. 'This is great. It feels like ages since we've had a proper sleepover all together.'

'Well, we had the drama trip, but that doesn't count.' Poppy shivers. 'Is Mrs Hargreaves the worst person in the world or what?'

We all laugh and nod in agreement.

'Was that the reason why you stopped coming to drama club?' Georgia asks me.

'Yeah.' I fiddle with my blanket. 'It was partly because of that day when Mrs Hargreaves told me that I speak too slowly. Because nobody said anything, I guess I just assumed that you agreed with her.'

The three of them jump up and come and sit nearer me. Georgia puts her arm around me.

'Why didn't you talk to us, Edie?' Poppy asks.

'I think I just felt a bit silly.'

'Nobody agreed with her,' Georgia says firmly. 'But we didn't want to speak for you.'

'You're always so chatty and happy and confident, we thought you'd be the one to speak up about it, or at least that you would speak to us about it,' Poppy admits.

'Sometimes it feels a bit tiring to always have to speak up about stuff though,' I say, 'and it was hard when we were having a terrible time. She was mean to all of us!'

'Am I really *that* bossy?' Poppy asks us quietly.

'You're you, and we wouldn't have it any other way,' I tell her.

Poppy grabs the bowl of Twiglets and offers them to me before taking one for herself. 'It's good to be honest. You should remember that, for yourself too!'

'Basically,' Chloe says, standing up as if she's about to deliver the closing statement in a courtroom, 'what we're saying is that we all had a truly terrible time on the trip.'

Poppy, Georgia and I nod in agreement. All week we've been telling Oscar and Pip about our miserable time on the trip.

'She doesn't know who we are! She *thinks* she knows us because she met us for, like, two seconds, but she has no idea.' Chloe holds up a Twiglet. 'This crisp knows me better than Mrs Hargreaves ever will!'

We grab a Twiglet each and cross them, as if we're knights crossing swords.

'Let's promise each other that if any of us feel sad or worried again, we'll talk about it.' Chloe looks around at all of us.

'Deal,' we agree.

We solemnly eat our Twiglets, as if that's a sign of our pact being sealed.

'Good. Now let's watch a scary movie!'

Oh no. Better get ready for the snacks to go EVERYWHERE.

Saturday 2.22pm

'I can't wait to show my mum my new football boots. They're going to bring me luck, I just know it,' Flora says as she skips out of the shop.

'I've never seen you so excited! Who knew some silly trainers would make you this happy?' I tease.

'Edie, they are not *trainers*, they're *football boots*, there's a big difference, and they're going to be the reason we're going to win on Tuesday. Are you still coming, by the way? I know football isn't your *favourite* thing ever, but I really like seeing you on the side, looking confused!'

I poke Flora and link arms with her. We head for the café we left Sara in. She was feeling a bit tired, so she decided to have a sit down and a cup of tea.

'Yes I am coming,' I told her. 'We're all coming! Georgia, Pip, Chloe, Oscar, Tom.'

'Not Poppy?'

I shake my head. 'Nothing will make Poppy stand outside watching football for two hours, no way!'

Flora laughs in agreement, and holds the café door

open for me. We walk up to Sara's table and see she's talking to another woman, who is standing over her. She's probably another one of Sara's friends. She loves talking and meeting new people – she's friends with practically the entire town.

As we get closer to the table, I realise that Flora has tensed up.

'Honestly, I'm fine,' Sara is telling the woman. 'I don't need help or company. My daughter and her friend have just popped to the shop and they'll be back soon.'

'It's no trouble,' the woman says in a silly high voice. It sounds like she's talking to a baby and not an adult woman. 'I will wait here with you in case you get confused or need help.'

'Hi, Mum,' Flora says sharply. She gives the woman a look that I've never seen her give before. She looks seriously angry.

'There we go then,' says Sara brightly. 'Here's my daughter! Thanks, bye.'

The woman looks at Flora and then back at Sara, as if she's judging the situation and seeing whether it's safe for her to leave. Eventually she goes back to sitting on the other side of the café.

'Why did you *thank* her, Mum?' Flora asks, sounding cross. I'm confused and I don't know whether Flora is angry at her mum, or the random woman. 'She was hassling you for no reason at all.'

'Flora, darling, how many times? People never mean any harm by it. They think they're doing something nice and helpful.'

'How can bugging somebody ever be seen as helpful? They see somebody in a wheelchair and assume they need help. Even if you tell them you don't!'

'I'd rather they bugged me every now and then rather than ignored people who actually *need* help.'

'Does it get annoying though, Sara?' I ask. I think about all the times when people ask me if I need help, or ask me silly questions, or patronise me, or speak to the people I'm with *about* me instead of speaking *to* me. 'Do you ever get so angry that you want to shout at them? Because I do.'

'Every situation is different, I guess, but all I know is if I got angry with every single person who treats me differently because I'm a wheelchair user, I'd spend too much of my life angry. Some things you've got to let wash over you. Choose your battles.'

Sara turns to Flora, who is still looking annoyed, and ruffles her hair. 'You hear that? Let it wash over you. Now show me your trainers.'

'They're not trainers, Sara, they're *football boots*,' I correct her, grinning at Flora.

Flora grins back, and pulls out the boots from the bag to show her mum.

Tuesday 5.48pm

There's a big group of us in the stand watching Flora play football. She's already scored two goals. If she scores another goal, she'll have scored what's called a 'hat-trick'. See? I know things about football and I am learning!

Her new football boots are definitely working!

When we reach the second half, it is a draw. 2–2.

'Two minutes extra time.' Oscar looks nervous. 'Come on, Flora! One more goal!'

Flora tackles a girl on the opposite side and gets the ball. She spins around and sprints down the pitch. It's brilliant.

Thirty more seconds until the referee blows their whistle.

I am now screaming so hard, I think I might lose my voice.

Oscar is shouting too and grabs my hand.

'COME ON, FLORA!'

Flora takes the shot, and the ball flies up in the air and curves, neatly, into the top left corner of the net.

'GOAL!'

Oscar grabs me and hugs me, just as the referee

blows the whistle for the end of the game.

She did it! Flora is at the other side of the pitch, hugging the other players. They lift her up in celebration and carry her over to us. She looks very happy, and a little bit embarrassed, I think because she's getting so much attention.

'Flora! Flora! Flora!' the rest of the team chant.

When she gets to our crowd, the players lower her and Flora hugs me.

'You did it, Flora, you won the game!' I tell her.

She looks into my eyes. And then she kisses me on my lips.

Maybe I *do* like football!

Thursday 4.58pm

It's the end of drama club and we're packing up.

'Oh, before you go,' Mr Murphy stops us, 'there's a drama trip in the summer term, to London. I'd love as many of you as possible to sign up.'

I put my coat on. London! I've been once, with my parents, but years ago. It would be Amazing with a capital A!

'We're going to see a few musicals and all the sights,'

I look round at my friends. Georgia and Poppy look as excited as I am.

Mr Murphy puts the props in the cupboard. 'We'll be going with Mrs Hargreaves and her drama group.'

I feel like I've been punched in the tummy. Why does Mrs Hargreaves have to go?

'I'll leave a piece of paper here and if you're interested in the London trip, just put your name down. I'll see you all next week!'

Mr Murphy grabs his bag and his coat and leaves.

'I'm not going anywhere with her!' Georgia says defiantly, crossing her arms.

The whole group look at the piece of paper. We think about it – and then turn and walk away.

Thursday 7.00pm

We have Louie's birthday dinner on
Grandad Eric's bed, so he doesn't miss
out on all the fun. We've had a buffet:
sausage rolls, Scotch eggs, mini pizzas
(margherita, naturally!), cheese and pineapple,
and, of course, Louie's
favourite, party rings. I
think Louie's had a few
too many party rings,
because his lips are coated
in sugar and he keeps jumping on Grandad
Eric's bed.

Mum holds the cake in the doorway and we sing
'Happy Birthday' to him.

Louie looks at his Smarties-covered birthday cake as
if it's the most precious thing in the whole world. He
scrambles over Grandad Eric to blow out his candles.

'Please can I blow them out again, Mummy?' he asks,
so sweetly. Mum rolls her eyes but lights them all again.
Mum has barely lit the last candle before Louie blows

them all out a second time.

'Louie, you need to be careful. Grandad Eric is still poorly,' Dad tells him.

'Oh there's absolutely nowt wrong with me any more, I'm right as rain. Angela,' he says, propping himself up with cushions, 'I don't suppose you could get me some hot sauce could you, to go with this sausage roll?'

'Dad, please tell me you're joking. What do I keep telling you? No more hot things, or else you'll end up in hospital again,' my mum warns him.

'It's just a little joke, love.' Grandad Eric assured her. 'Now, when will you let me go back home? I'm bored of you lot.'

I know Grandad Eric is only joking, but I think Louie believes him, because he pulls his bottom lip out, as if he is about to cry.

'Please, Grandad Eric, please don't leave us. I like living with you. I like our evening disco dances.'

'I like it too,' I agree. I will miss being able to come into his room and talk to him whenever I want.

Grandad Eric holds both his arms out and me and Louie wriggle up the bed until we're next to him.

'I will miss you both too, so much. But you'll see me all the time. Like you did before. I can drive you to school, and I'll be round for tea every week, like normal. But maybe minus the hot stuff!'

'Good!' my mum sings. 'Now, who wants the last sausage roll?'

'Me!' Louie jumps up and grabs it right out of her hand. 'I like being five. I already feel taller!'

'That might be because you're standing on a bed, Lou!' I suggest.

'Oh yeah,' he giggles.

Friday 1.05pm

It's Friday lunchtime, and we're all sitting in our usual spot, eating sandwiches, while Oscar and Flora continue to talk about football.

I think about all the brilliant adults I've talked to recently. Grandad Eric, my dad, Sara, Mrs Adler in the supermarket. They all gave me great pieces of advice, but how can I put them to good use?

Thursday 4.05pm

'Does anybody want to explain to me why nobody signed up to the drama trip next term?'

Mr Murphy holds up the empty piece of paper for the theatre trip and I can't tell if he's angry, sad or disappointed.

The whole group look around at each other and shift from side to side.

I think about speaking up, but then I remember when I tried to tell him about Mrs Hargreaves during the drama trip. He was quick to side with her and I'm guessing that he would probably do the same today.

Even Poppy, who is usually the spokesperson for us all, is quiet. Since the sleepover, I can tell that she is trying to speak less, and be less 'bossy'. That's a shame because it's my favourite thing about her. She is brilliant at taking charge of situations and it makes me sad that Mrs Hargreaves has made her doubt herself.

'Right, well, if nobody will speak to me about it,

I guess we'll move on then, shall we?'

Mr Murphy sighs, and puts down the paper.

Thursday 6.23pm

It's parents' evening. It's the first time that my mum and dad have met my teachers and I think it's going quite well. Most of the teachers have said that I'm good in class, but sometimes I get carried away and I chat too much.

'Bit like your mum then,' Dad prods me, as we walk from desk to desk.

I look over and see Oscar and his parents speaking to Miss Jamison, the art teacher. He's gone bright red. He totally fancies her . . . how funny!

'Right, where's our last stop?' Mum asks, looking down at her form. 'Ah, your favourite, English.'

We look for Mr Messer and we see him sitting at a desk in the corner of the room. When we approach his table he stands up and shakes both my mum and my dad's hands. We sit down opposite him.

'Well, what can I say about Edie? In a word, she's brilliant,' Mr Messer asks, 'Her creative writing is astounding. The best in the class.'

'She wants to be a writer,' Mum says proudly, 'so

that's very good to hear.'

Mr Messer nods. Then he looks quite serious. 'The only matter of concern is the little blip earlier this year, with Edie not completing her homework.'

My stomach tightens, as if there's a rope in my tummy that is being pulled from two opposite sides.

'It was disappointing, especially because the grade goes towards Edie's Speaking and Listening mark for the year. Because she never completed this assignment, I'm afraid that her overall grade will be affected.'

'Yes, we were sad to hear about that too,' Dad says. Mum is quiet. I don't know what to say to make the situation better.

'Is there still time for Edie to hand in the assignment, or is it too late?' Dad asks.

Mr Messer looks thoughtful. 'I think we could manage that,' he says. 'Yes, if Edie can get it to me by the end of term, I'd be happy to grade it and put it towards her overall mark for the year.'

'Thank you, sir,' my mum says, and we stand up and begin to walk out of the hall.

'Edie, are these your parents?' a voice behind us asks.

We turn around to discover that it is Mr Murphy. Great. As if tonight couldn't get any worse. 'Please could I have a word with you before you go?'

Mr Murphy leads us to his table and we sit down. I have no idea what he is going to say.

'Now, although I am not strictly speaking one of Edie's teachers, I do spend a lot of time with her in drama club, and I want to firstly say how incredibly proud and impressed I was with her performance last term at the Christmas play. Edie, truly, you were great.'

'Thank you, sir,' I say nervously, not knowing what is coming.

'But lately, Edie, I haven't felt like your heart is in drama as much as it was. You didn't come to drama for most of this term . . .'

'What?' Mum asks. 'Edie, you didn't tell me that. Where have you been going?'

I shrug. 'I just went to Flora's house and hung out with her and Sara for a bit. I didn't want to go to drama for a while. But I've started going again, so don't worry, it's all fine.'

'That's true,' says Mr Murphy gently, 'but you seem

much quieter than usual. And you haven't signed up for the London drama trip. Is this because of what happened on the trip at half-term?'

'Why, what happened on the drama trip?' Mum asks, now sounding quite concerned.

I shuffle in my seat. 'It was nothing, Mum,' I say. 'I just didn't get on with one of the teachers, and I didn't have a nice time. She said some things.'

'What things?' Dad asks gently. He doesn't sound as concerned as Mum, which makes me feel better.

'She didn't want me to have a part with many lines,' I hesitate slightly, 'because she said I would take too long. Because I speak slowly.'

Mr Murphy visibly tenses. 'Is that what she said?' he asks. I nod.

There is a silence.

'And is this why you stopped coming to the group?'

I nod, feeling ashamed.

'Edie, I am so sorry that happened to you, and I wish you could have told me.'

'I tried to, sir, but I didn't know how. It wasn't just what she said to me, she made everybody's week miserable. We all hated it.'

'Which is why none of you want to go on the trip. Because she'll be there.' Mr Murphy says, as if everything suddenly made sense.

'But why didn't you talk to us?' Mum asks me. 'You used to talk to us about everything.'

'Because she's a grown-up, and I thought she might be right. Maybe I shouldn't be a performer because of the way I talk. Or maybe I should. I don't know. I don't know a lot of things right now. And I feel like the older I get, the less I actually know. I know that doesn't make sense at all, but it's how I feel right now.'

My parents and Mr Murphy look at me, and I suddenly feel like I've said something wrong. It feels like about two hours before somebody says something.

'Just because she's an adult, it doesn't condone what she said to you,' Mr Murphy says at last. He looks at my parents. 'I had no idea that this had happened and I can assure you the school will take this further.' Mum and Dad nod.

I thank Mr Murphy. The three of us stand up and leave the hall.

'Well, that was a rollercoaster,' Dad tries to joke when we get in the car.

I think about the conversation we had with Mr Messer, and then the conversation we had with Mr Murphy.

'There's so many things you haven't told us, Edie.' Mum sighs. 'Why? We had no idea about the trip. And why didn't you do your English assignment?'

'I didn't know what to say about the trip, Mum, and I didn't want you to worry. And with Mr Messer's assignment, he asked us to do a presentation about who I am. How can I do that when I don't *know* who I am? Life is so confusing.'

To my surprise, Mum and Dad start laughing. I don't understand why.

'Oi! What's so funny?' I ask them.

'You've nailed life right there, Edie, my love,' Mum says softly. 'Life *is* confusing.'

'And it never stops being confusing,' Dad agrees.

Oh, great.

But I suddenly feel ready to complete Mr Messer's homework. I have one more weekend before the Easter break, and I am determined to give in my homework to him before the end of term. Even though it's two million years late!

Saturday 1.30pm

The doorbell rings, and Mum comes into the kitchen holding a parcel.

'Parcel for Miss Eckhart.'

'That'll be more Post-it Notes. Could you pop them down there? Thank you, love you, Mum,'

I have taken over the kitchen table with different coloured pens, glitter and Post-it Notes.

'Love you too. Are you sure I can't help you?' She looks at my different coloured piles, scattered over the table and frowns. 'It looks very . . . complex.'

'I'm good, Mum. I need to do this on my own. I just hope Mr Messer will like it.'

Mum kisses me on the top of my head, 'I'm sure he will.'

Tuesday 10.02am

I feel nervous in English class. People are still coming into the classroom, but I decide that it is best to get it out of the way, so I put my hand up tall until Mr Messer notices me.

'Yes, Edie?'

'Erm, I just wanted to tell you that I have done my homework. The presentation about who I am.'

Mr Messer smiles, looking relieved. 'That's excellent news, Edie. Do you want to do it today, in front of the class?'

I nod, and as soon as everybody has sat down, Mr Messer stands up and starts the class.

'Morning team! It's the last English lesson before the Easter holidays, so we have a little treat. Edie didn't manage to do her 'Who Am I?' assignment with the rest of you, but the good news is she's going to present to us today.'

'Good luck!' Pip whispers, holding up her two thumbs. I pick up all of my Post-it Notes and I make my way to the front of the class. I feel so nervous, I can feel my heartbeat in my mouth.

'Hello,' I begin, 'my name is Edie.'

I pick up the first Post-it Note. It has the name 'Edie' written on it. I stick it on my chest.

'I am a daughter, a granddaughter and a sister. My brother calls me "Didi".'

I pick up the next four Post-it Notes: 'daughter', 'granddaughter', 'sister' and 'Didi' and place them on my jumper.

'I love talking, and I get very excited very easily. Sometimes people describe me as loud.'

I place the 'loud' Post-it Note on me.

'But sometimes I like to sit and think on my own and write. And then some people describe me as quiet.'

Next to the 'loud' note, I then stick a 'quiet' Post-it Note.

'I write poems and short stories, but then I also love acting. In the Christmas play I played Scrooge and I loved it.'

I add two more Post-it Notes to my jumper: 'writer' and 'actor'.

I continue, until my entire jumper is covered in

different Post-it Notes. Some contradict each other, but all are ways to describe me, and things I like, and things I enjoy doing.

I look down at my jumper. 'That's a lot of ways to describe one person and some days I don't feel like all of these labels quite fit me. This time next week I'll probably have ten new labels to stick on, and sometimes that is confusing and scary. It's why I put off doing this presentation, because I was scared to be honest.'

I place the last two Post-it Notes on myself: 'scared' and 'honest'.

'But then I realised,' I begin to take all of the Post-it Notes off, one by one, until I am left with just one, 'none of these labels matter, as long as I'm Edie. That's who I am. I am Edie, and that is enough.'

I grab my notebook and open it.

'Here's a poem I have written. It's called, "Things I Don't Know".

I clear my throat, and I suddenly don't feel nervous
any more.

'I don't know what I'll look like when I'm older.
I don't know whether I'll have grey hair and
wrinkles on my head.
I don't know where I'll be living.
And I don't know whether my favourite colour
will still be red.

I don't know whether I'll learn how to drive.
I don't know what my job will be.
I don't know whether I'll fall in love.
And I don't know who I will marry.

I don't know whether the world will change for
the better,
I don't know whether the world will change for
the worse,
I don't know how many kids I will have,
And I don't know how to end this verse.

But I do know that I like who I am,
And I love my friends and family,
I am enough and I am proud of who I am.
Because it's OK to simply be "me".'

Wednesday 1.02pm

'Honestly, I wish you could've seen it. Edie got a standing ovation! In class! It was seriously, seriously cool,' Pip tells the gang at lunch.

I laugh and say, 'Luckily Mr Messer kinda ignored the fact that it was, like, two months late!'

'I wish we could've seen it,' Oscar says. 'It sounds great!'

I feel relieved to have finally done the homework and being honest with the class wasn't as scary as I thought it was going to be.

There's just one more thing I need to do to put right everything that has happened this term.

'Is everyone free on Saturday? For an end-of-term sleepover at my house?' I ask.

Everybody nods and says it sounds brilliant.

Great!

Saturday 7.05pm

Me and my friends are sitting in a circle on the grass in my garden.

'Welcome, Oscar. Tonight you're an honorary member of drama club. I thought, because we all had such a terrible time on the trip, I'd like to put it right. This is our chance to do the play again, the way we want to,'

'I don't have to act again, do I?' Flora asks, looking concerned.

'Absolutely not.' I grab her hand and squeeze it. 'You are in charge of the set. I've got some cardboard boxes and some paints over there.'

Flora beams and heads to the bottom of the garden to crack on with the painting.

'I have arranged plugs, straighteners and curlers for you, Georgia, and you have as long as you need to do your hair.'

Georgia looks at the bottom corner of the garden and sees a little hairdressing station set up. She squeals with joy.

'And now I'm not quite sure what we should do next,

so I thought, Poppy, you should take charge.'

'Are you sure?' she asks me. 'I don't want to take charge, and be, erm, bossy.'

'You're not bossy, you're a leader, and right now we need you to lead the play.'

Poppy claps her hands together with glee. 'Right, let's put on the best garden play ever!'

For the next few hours, we laugh and play around. We decide to write our own play about our drama trip, with Chloe playing Mrs Hargreaves, because she is the only one of us that she didn't insult!

All of the play is true and includes all of the rubbish things Mrs Hargreaves said to us during the week, but we decide to write our own ending.

One by one, we stand up to Mrs Hargreaves.

Flora tells her that she doesn't need to 'come out of her shell', she knows who she is, and she likes her shell!

Poppy tells her that she isn't 'bossy', she's a leader!

Georgia tells her that even though she cares about what she looks like, it doesn't mean that she is silly or an airhead.

Finally, I tell her that I don't talk too slowly, I talk at

'Edie speed', which is exactly the right speed for me.

When it gets darker, we invite my parents and Louie to watch the play. Oscar plays the part of the usher and shows them to their seats, and sells them ice cream at the interval.

Everybody loves it.

'That was brilliant, Edie,' Mum cheers. 'Now, it's almost midnight – bed!'

As if the night couldn't get any better, we are camping outside, together in a big tent.

'This is the best drama trip ever!' Georgia squeals.

I feel so lucky to call these people my friends.

☆☆☆

I don't know what time it is but I know it is late. I can't sleep. I'm too happy and excited after our great night.

I look over at Oscar and he is snoring away. Typical. He can lits sleep anywhere.

'Edie, are you still awake?' Flora asks me.

'Yes, I just keep thinking about tonight. I loved it.'

Even though it's quite dark, I can see that Flora is

smiling. 'Me too. You've had a brilliant week, putting things right. I'm proud of you. And you might not know exactly who you are, but I do. You're amazing, Edie Eckhart.'

My butterflies in my tummy fly around. It is suddenly the right time.

I reach inside the pocket of my pyjamas and pull out my last Post-it Note.

'I didn't put this in my presentation, but it is something I'd like to be, and I wasn't sure if you wanted it too.'

I hand the note to Flora and she opens it.

'Will you be my girlfriend?' I ask her.

'Yes,' she says, kissing me gently on my cheek. 'I will.'

Acknowledgements

Nobody writes a book on their own, and I could only write *The Amazing Edie Eckhart: The Big Trip* because I am surrounded by so many brilliant, talented people who keep me happy, strong and make me feel very loved.

As ever, thank you to my editor Polly Lyall Grant and my copyeditor Genevieve Herr for being incredible, and my greatest cheerleaders . . . I loved seeing how excited you were to find out what happens to Edie and Flora in this book!

To Flo, Lily, Helps and everybody at Off The Kerb for believing in me and running my life much better than I can. I don't know what I'd do without you all. Please can we go out for celebration cocktails soon?

To all of my friends and family. Thank you for understanding when I cancel on you, thank you for making me laugh until I stop breathing for a full minute, and thank you for joining me for gorgeous food and excellent nights out. I feel so lucky to have so many brilliant people in my life. I am so full of love.

To all the girls I have had crushes on in my life. Some of you know who you are and some of you probably have no idea that I had a crush on you! Maybe I can be as brave as Flora next year and give out my own handmade Valentine's card . . .

And most importantly, thank you to ALL OF YOU. Thank you for reading the first book in your classes, thank you for stopping me in the street to tell me how much you enjoyed reading about Edie, and thank you for dressing up as her for World Book Day. This has been the best year.

Stay tuned for Book 3!

Have you read the first book in the series?

THE AMAZING **EDIE ECKHART**

Being a little **wobbly** won't stop her...

ROSIE JONES

ILLUSTRATED BY NATALIE SMILLIE

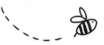

ROSIE JONES Is a comedian, actor and scriptwriter, who has cerebral palsy. Rosie is a regular on popular comedy shows including *The Last Leg*, *Mock the Week*, *8 Out of 10 Cats Does Countdown* and *Hypothetical*.

Rosie has written for *Sex Education* and hosts the podcast *Daddy Look at Me* with Helen Bauer. Rosie is incredibly excited to be a children's author – Jacqueline Wilson is her personal hero!